ADVANCE PRAISE FOR
Catching Christmas

"Blackstock's *Catching Christmas* is not your average romance. Darling and laugh-out-loud cute, it makes the reader think about the important things in life. I read it in one gulp and wished there was more. Highly recommended!"

> —Colleen Coble, *USA TODAY* bestselling author of the Hope Beach and Lavender Tides series

"The feel-good Christmas book of the year. Blackstock's tale of love and redemption wrapped in a holiday bow will leave you smiling. Don't miss *Catching Christmas*."

> —Rachel Hauck, *New York Times* bestselling author of *The Wedding Dress* and *The Love Letter*

"Terri Blackstock's latest offering touches tender places with its quirky characters and stirring plot. *Catching Christmas* explores what happens when the paths of a disenchanted taxi driver collide with that of an over-worked attorney. Blackstock weaves a compelling, romantic tale that is sure to get you into the Christmas spirit!"

> —Denise Hunter, bestselling author of *Honeysuckle Dreams* and *A December Bride*

Praise for Terri Blackstock

"*If I Live* is a grabber from page one, delivering an exhilarating mix of chase, mystery, and spiritual truth. Longtime Blackstock fans will be delighted, and new Blackstock fans will be made."

—James Scott Bell, bestselling author of
the Mike Romeo thrillers

"Blackstock proves once again that she is the queen of Christian suspense in this third and final installment of the If I Run series."

—*CBA Market* for *If I Live*

"Wow! What an ending to Casey Cox's edge-of-your seat quest for justice! Unputdownable from start to finish, this novel will keep readers glued to the page, ignoring anything else they may have planned for the day, until they've fully absorbed every twist and turn."

—*RT Book Reviews*, 4 1/2 stars,
TOP PICK! for *If I Live*

"In Blackstock's stirring conclusion . . . Readers of Christian romantic suspense will find much to like."

—*Publishers Weekly* for *If I Live*

"Emotions, tensions, and suspense all run high in this fast-paced, edge-of-your-seat thriller. The continuing storyline in

Blackstock's If I Run series keeps readers hungrily devouring each new book and waiting impatiently for the next."

—*RT Book Reviews*, 4½ stars,
TOP PICK! for *If I'm Found*

"With nimble use of alternating viewpoints, Blackstock has delivered a fine follow-up to *If I Run* that ratchets up the tension for the final installment."

—*Publishers Weekly* for *If I'm Found*

"Crisp dialogue and unexpected twists make this compulsive reading, and a final chapter cliffhanger leaves things poised for a sequel."

—*Publishers Weekly* for *If I Run*

"A fast-paced, thoroughly mesmerizing thriller, *If I Run* offers distinct Christian undertones. Though not preachy, this layering adds to the complexity of this suspenseful novel. An enthralling read with an entirely unexpected conclusion makes the reader question if a sequel could be in the works."

—*NY Journal of Books*

"Blackstock's newest novel, *If I Run*, is the best suspense novel I've read in decades. Boiling with secrets, nail-biting suspense, and exquisitely developed characters, it's a story that grabs hold and never lets go. Read this one. Run to get it! It's that good."

—Colleen Coble, *USA Today* bestselling author of
Mermaid Moon and the Hope Beach series

Catching Christmas

Other Books by Terri Blackstock

Catching Christmas

TERRI BLACKSTOCK

THOMAS NELSON
Since 1798

Catching Christmas

Published in Nashville, Tennessee, by Thomas Nelson. Thomas Nelson is a registered trademark of HarperCollins Christian Publishing, Inc.

Thomas Nelson titles may be purchased in bulk for educational, business, fund-raising, or sales promotional use. For information, please e-mail SpecialMarkets@ThomasNelson.com.

Scripture quotations are taken from the New American Standard Bible®, Copyright © 1960, 1962, 1963, 1968, 1971, 1972, 1973, 1975, 1977, 1995 by The Lockman Foundation. Used by permission. (www.Lockman.org)

Publisher's Note: This novel is a work of fiction. Names, characters, places, and incidents are either products of the author's imagination or used fictitiously. All characters are fictional, and any similarity to people living or dead is purely coincidental.

ISBN 978-0-310-35173-3 (e-book)

Library of Congress Cataloging-in-Publication Data

Names: Blackstock, Terri, 1957- author.
Title: Catching Christmas / Terri Blackstock.
Description: Nashville : Thomas Nelson, [2018]
Identifiers: LCCN 2018008671 | ISBN 9780310351726 (hard cover)
Subjects: LCSH: Christmas stories.
Classification: LCC PS3552.L34285 C38 2018 | DDC 813/.54--dc23 LC record available at https://lccn.loc.gov/2018008671

Printed in the United States of America

18 19 20 21 22 LSC 5 4 3 2 1

*This book is lovingly dedicated
to the Nazarene.*

CHAPTER 1

Finn

I'm not a violent man, but I have a dozen reasons for pulling my cab over and throwing the chattering man in my back seat onto the curb. His cheesy Christmas outfit is one of them. His love affair with Uber is another.

"Not trying to insult you or anything," the man says. "But I don't see why any of you are still working for cab companies. The Uber model is the wave of the future, don't you think? I mean, seriously, it's so convenient for consumers, with the app charging your credit card and everything. And you don't have that blasted meter staring you in the face . . ."

I look at the man in the rearview mirror. "You got money or not?"

"Of course. What do you mean?"

"You sound like a guy who has a problem handing a credit card or cash to an actual human being. You'd rather put it in an app where who knows who in India or China or somewhere is saving all your data."

The man's laughter is defensive and unnatural. "How old are you?" he asks. "You don't look old enough to be suspicious of the Internet. You look like that guy Luke on *Gilmore Girls*. My wife would love you. You probably get that a lot."

"Never heard of the guy," I say, even though I get it at least once a week.

"The way he looked at the end of the series."

The older version, of course. I'm feeling older all the time, even though I only turned thirty a month ago.

I'm getting close to the guy's destination, something I know since I have intimate knowledge of the St. Louis street map without a GPS, so it isn't worth responding.

But the guy loves the sound of his voice. "I only

took a cab because it's raining and it's rush hour. Uber spikes their prices up at times like this. And there you were, sitting at the hotel where my convention was . . ."

Now I have to respond. "So you'd rather ride with some dude who hasn't had as many background checks as I have, who doesn't have to pay the same license fees and taxes, who doesn't know how to get where you're going unless he's looking at his phone while he's trying to drive, who might have been working in a lab for his day job, where he handles live viruses and doesn't believe in washing his hands—"

"Come on," the guy says. "That's ridiculous."

"Most ride-share drivers don't do it for a living, pal. I know the shortcuts—"

"But you don't take them. Come on, you know cabs go out of their way to run up the bill. Those drivers may not do it for a living, but they're good enough. And I usually know where I'm going. I can tell them how to get there."

"You know," I cut back in, "that's another thing. *Good enough* is really what you want? How about excellence? You watch TV on six-inch devices, you read your news on blogs, you eat fast food rather than cooking. You're happier with two all-beef patties than you are with fine restaurants or—here's a concept—home-cooked meals."

The guy leans forward on the seat, and I fight my urge to shove him back. "What is your problem?" he asks. "What does my diet have to do with driving a cab?"

Nothing, but it has everything to do with me. I'm seriously losing it. I'll never make it through this Christmas season.

I reach the guy's destination, and pulling over to the curb, I check the meter. "Eight bucks," I say. "Do you want a receipt?"

The guy doesn't move. "I asked you a question."

I turn and look back at him. "You want me to keep that meter running?"

The guy shakes his head, pulls out his wallet, and hands me a ten. "Give me a receipt, since I don't have it on an app."

I'm pretty sure the guy doesn't intend to tip me, so I fish two dollars out of my pouch and hand them back to him with a receipt. The guy snatches them and opens his door.

"Want my card?" I shout after him.

He slams the door, and I chuckle as I drive away.

You run into jerks in every line of work. Unfortunately, I meet more than my share, especially this time of year, when there are Christmas parties every single day.

My radio crackles, and my dispatcher comes on.

"Finn, where are you?"

"Northwest," I say. "What you got?"

"Someone in that area called for a cab. Address is 113 Sensero Drive."

I groan at the address. "Come on, LuAnn, that's a residential neighborhood. I was going back to the airport."

"You're the closest. I was supposed to book this earlier, but I didn't."

Why didn't the person call Uber? It's getting rare for people who aren't accustomed to looking up a phone number to call the cab company. And they love to watch the progress of their Uber drivers on their phones, which I consider another way the government can keep tabs on us. Just sign up to drive for a ride-share company, and you, too, can be tracked anywhere and everywhere.

Most of my fares these days are airport or hotel fares, and those are the easiest. Sure money, sure pickups, and not a lot of time lost waiting for someone. As irritating as those fares can be if they've been drinking, they pay my rent.

But occasionally we get a call from an actual house. It's usually someone who doesn't know how to use a smartphone. Those can be the most irritating fares.

I do what I hate and type the address into my dashboard GPS, since I refuse to do it on my phone as a matter of principle. I follow the voice guidance as I drive.

It's a white ranch-style house that looks like it needs a good coat of paint. The grass could use a mow. They probably aren't big tippers. Great.

I tap my horn and watch the door. There's no sign of anybody, but I see through the screen door that the front door is open. As I wait, I turn on the radio and scan through "I Saw Mommy Kissing Santa Claus," "Santa Baby," and Michael Jackson's version of "Santa Claus Is Coming to Town." It's been all Christmas, all the time, since Thanksgiving. I wonder if these oblivious station managers really think that if they take a break and play a Top 40 song people will flee in search of more "Jingle Bells."

Time is wasting. I'm going to the door. Try getting an Uber driver to do that.

I straighten my backward baseball cap and go to the screen door. I make sure my knock conveys my impatience. When no one answers, I move closer to the screen and look inside.

An old woman sits in a wheelchair, her head tilted forward. Either she's sleeping or she's dead. Great.

I look back at my cab. I could tell LuAnn that no one came to the door, which is true. I could just drive off, but the woman will probably wake up and call back and complain that no one came.

I knock again on the screen door. "Hello?" I yell.

The woman jolts awake. "What?"

"Did someone here call for a cab?"

The woman looks around, as if she doesn't know if anyone else is there who may have called. "Yes . . . uh . . . oh yes. Thank you so much."

"Do you need help?"

"Yes, please. That would be so nice."

I open the screen door and step into the small front room. Her purse sits on the table, so I point to it. "Do you need your purse?"

"Please," she says.

I wheel her out the door, carrying her purse. "Should I lock it?"

"Yes, thank you."

I lock the doorknob and pull it shut.

The woman reminds me a little of my own mother in her last days, and that familiar bitter acid burns my stomach. I roll her to the car.

"Uh . . . can you stand up or walk?"

"With a little help," she says. "My name's Callie. What's yours, honey?"

"Finn," I say, folding up her footrests so she can reach the ground. I help her up. She's very weak as she takes one step, then falls purposefully onto the car seat. I wait for her to pull her feet in, but she just stays there with them hanging outside the car. Sighing, I bend down, pick up her feet, and put them into the car.

I close her door and load the wheelchair into the trunk. When I get behind the wheel, I start the meter, wishing I could add the fifteen minutes it took me to get her into the blasted car. "Where are you going, ma'am?"

She doesn't answer, so I look back at her. She's already asleep again. Unbelievable.

So where am I supposed to take her? I call LuAnn back on the radio. "Hey, this fare I just picked up at 113 Sensero Drive? Did she tell you where she wanted to go?"

"Yeah," she says. "She wanted to go to a doctor's appointment at St. Mary's Hospital. Her appointment is at two."

"Okay, thanks." I look back at her again and realize she isn't belted in. She'll probably fall over when I start moving. Sighing, I get out and go around the car, hook her seat belt.

I pull away from the curb. At the first intersection, I glance in the rearview. She does fall forward, but the belt holds her body up.

Is she sick? She looks as frail as a toothpick, and she has to be in her nineties. What kind of family would leave her to get to the doctor on her own? Isn't there someone who could have done this for her?

It only takes a few minutes to get to the hospital. I go to the clinic wing and pull up to the entrance. She's still sleeping, so I go around to her door. I bend over and unclick her seat belt. "Ma'am? We're here."

She comes awake and looks up at me with vacant eyes. "What?"

"We're here."

"Where?"

"The doctor's office. You have an appointment at two. This is the place, right?"

"I . . . I'm not sure. Heavens, I don't know where my manners are."

"Your manners?"

"Yes. I'm Callie. And you are?"

"The cab driver."

"Oh," she says.

"It's six-fifty," I say a little too loudly, assuming she's hard of hearing. "I'll get your wheelchair."

She has ten dollars in her hand when I come back. I shove it into my pocket, then help her into the chair. "Ma'am, can you get yourself to the office?"

"What office?"

"The doctor's office. This is the clinic where your appointment is."

She looks toward the building. Zero sign of

comprehension. Nada. She could be going into a movie theater for all she knows.

"Can you wheel yourself? Or do you need me to push you in there?"

"That would be so nice," she says. "I'm Callie. And who are you?"

"Finn." I slam the door a little too hard and lock it even though it's still running. My luck, some patient doped up on painkillers will hijack it and try to fly with it. Hopefully I can get back before someone lobs a brick through the window.

I roll her through the doors. "Do you remember who your doctor is?"

Of course she doesn't. She looks confused and opens her purse, sifts through for something.

"Ma'am? Your doctor?"

When she doesn't find whatever she's looking for, I push her toward the check-in desk. "Ma'am, what's your last name?" I ask her.

"Callie Beecher," she says.

"I'm Finn," I say quickly before she can ask me again. I have to wait in line as patients before me sign in with the slowest scrawls I can imagine.

Callie gradually comes alive as she looks around

at all the people in line. She taps the young woman standing in front of her. "I used to have hair that color." Her voice is loud, commanding attention. "Red on the head, they used to say. Do they say that to you?"

"No, ma'am."

"My granddaughter has hair that color, but she dyes it blonde. My daughter's wasn't red, though. Hers was naturally blonde, thankfully."

Past tense. The woman must have outlived her daughter.

"She cried when her baby had red hair," she drones on. "She said redheads are hideous. I tried not to take it personal."

The girl looks graciously amused. "She said that?"

Callie's expression goes blank for a moment, and I'm pretty sure she's lost her train of thought. She looks around, then her gaze settles on the girl again. She stares at her for a moment, as if it's the first time she's seen her. "You won't be winning any beauty contests, but I think you're pretty."

"Thank you." The girl clearly has a sense of humor—she grins at those gasping and chuckling around her. In spite of my irritation, I can't help grinning, too.

A nurse who hasn't missed many meals comes out a side door and calls to the next patient.

Callie notices her, then looks over at the red-head. In a voice way too loud for the room, she says, "Are my thighs that big?"

The nurse turns, fire in her eyes, but when she sees that the person insulting her is older than Methuselah, she just shakes her head. Everyone around us stifles a grin.

"No, ma'am," the redhead giggles.

"I used to have cable TV," Callie goes on, "and I would watch that show about the chubby nurse. What was her name?"

The girl is losing control of her giggles now, and tears are surfacing in her eyes. "I don't know."

"She had a pretty face, though."

I don't make eye contact with Callie for fear she'll try to pull me into her lunacy.

Finally, the person in front of us is finished, and I move to the front. The bored receptionist looks up at me. "Help you?"

"Yes, I have Callie Beecher here to see the doctor."

"Which doctor?"

"I don't know."

"We have thirty doctors here."

I lean over the desk. "Can you look her up? She's having some memory problems."

The woman types in the name. "Her appointment is with Dr. Patrick. Wait over there and they'll call her."

"She might be a little hard of hearing, and she falls asleep a lot, so you might need to go get her when they call her."

The receptionist looks like she couldn't care less, but she gives me a noncommittal nod.

I push Callie to the waiting area, lock her wheelchair, and bend toward her. "Ma'am, here's my card. If you need me to come back and get you when you're done, just call this number."

The middle-aged woman sitting next to her looks at me like I'm pond scum. "You're leaving her alone?"

"Lady, I'm just the cab driver."

"Oh."

"Her name's Callie Beecher. Would you keep an ear out for them to call her?"

"Yes, if they don't call me first."

I look down at Callie. "Ma'am, you put that card somewhere where you can find it again, okay?"

I glance through the glass wall into my law firm's conference room. Half of the meeting's attendees are already there, though they're hardly aware of each other since most of them are focused on their phones. I hear voices up the hall, and I see the partners walking in a pack toward me—just as a woman picks up at the other end of my call.

"Hello, this is Sandra, the nurse. The doctor's in with a patient. Can I help you?"

"I've already talked to you, Sandra," I say, lowering my voice to almost a whisper. "I asked you to have him call me, and you didn't."

"I'm sorry, I'm having trouble hearing you."

The partners are lingering at the door, not three feet from me. I have to get in there now. "You already have a message from me to give him. Please give it to him. If he calls me I'll try to answer. Please. It's important I talk to him as soon as possible."

I click off the phone, plaster a smile on my face, and greet my bosses as I slip into the room. I take my place among the other first-year associates, who suddenly look engaged as the heavyweights enter the room. My friend Joanie has saved me a chair next to her, too close to the Christmas tree decorated by the priciest interior decorator in town. The heat of the incandescent lights is going to make me sweat.

"Did she get there?" Joanie whispers behind her hand as I sit down.

"Who knows? If the cab company didn't send someone, I'm suing them."

"I covered for you at lunch. They don't know you were late."

"Thanks. I had to get her dressed. She was still in her pajamas."

"You have got to get help for her."

"I know, but I can't afford it."

The meeting comes to order, and I try to focus on the senior partner who's presiding—the Southerby in Southerby, Maddox, and Hanes. But my mind keeps wandering to my grandmother who was staring into space last night in front of her hours-old Meals on Wheels lunch, which she hadn't touched.

Her decline in the last few days has been so rapid. Maybe it's just some virus that has made her seem worse than she is, or maybe she isn't sleeping well. I was going to take her to the doctor today myself, but then the partners called this meeting for the exact same time as the appointment. I couldn't risk missing it.

Mr. Southerby is twirling an unlit cigarette in his fingers as he talks. His heart attack last year scared him into quitting, but he still carries one wherever he goes. "And as you know," he continued, "billing has been down in the last quarter. We blame a couple of lawsuits that didn't come out in our favor, and a few lost clients due to Benedict Simon's leaving the firm."

Everyone chuckles at the "Benedict" part of the name, because Simon's real name is Larry. His leaving with some major clients has made the partners bitter.

"Long story short, we tell you this with great regret, but we are going to be downsizing our staff, and that means we'll be letting a few of our first-year associates go."

I gasp. He has my full attention now. I look at the others around me. Everyone is gaping at him, waiting for the ax to fall. "We'll be calling some of you into meetings this afternoon and letting you know whether you'll be kept on or let go. Those of you who stay on will have to step it up. You'll obviously be doing the work of two or three people, so if you can't handle that, perhaps you should go ahead and step down."

Is he looking at me as he says that, or is that just my imagination? I roll my chair back a few inches, hoping the flashing tree will hide me.

What am I going to do if they fire me?

When the meeting is over, the partners leave first, probably so they won't be ambushed in the hall. Some of the associates get up and follow them out, no doubt hoping to convince them that they're indispensable to the team. I sit frozen, staring at the air in front of me.

"It's going to be me," I tell Joanie, who's also paralyzed beside me. "He was looking at me when he said that thing about stepping down if you didn't think you could hack it."

"But if you were getting fired, there wouldn't be anything to step down from. Besides, I thought he was looking at me."

"Why would he look at you? You haven't been coming in late because you can't get your grandmother bathed and dressed on time, no matter how early you get there, because something always goes wrong."

"But maybe they know I've been covering for you. Maybe they're madder at me than they are at you. You're more valuable, after all. You did good work on the Krieleg case, and they were awarded a hundred million dollars. We lost the last case I went to court on. Plus you're on the Darco case. They're not going to fire you the day before you go to court."

I sigh. "It's the stupidest case in the history of lawsuits, which is guaranteed to ruin my reputation whether I win or lose."

"If you win, it will make our biggest client happy."

"Get real. Everyone knows this is a losing battle. His kid provides the alcohol for a dorm party, then smashes his car into a Burger King after he gets wasted, so the kid sues the school for allowing him to get that drunk. And when I finish this one, I get to represent this stellar young man as he sues Burger King."

"Like I said, job security. Stupid cases have been won before."

"But any of us could work on this case and get the same result." I blow out a frustrated breath and take a quick inventory of my accomplishments here because I may need to remind the partners of them.

It doesn't seem like enough, and some of the other first-years have been so much more successful. "And anyway, I was a second on the Krieleg case. I don't get the credit."

"You worked day and night, and most of what they used in court was stuff you found. They're not going to let you go."

"Then who?"

"I don't know. They didn't even say how many. I'm gonna be sick." Joanie slides her chair back and stands up.

She does look pale. I watch her leave the room, then I look toward the podium again, trying to remember exactly what Mr. Southerby was saying when he glanced toward me. Was it really the "can't commit to long hours" part?

I can't just sit here. I have a million things to do before court tomorrow, and I have to keep working as if I'm valuable to someone. I make myself get out of my chair and leave the room. For a minute I stand in the hallway as though I don't know how to find my office. What is wrong with me? I have to be on top of my game.

As I walk, I look down at my phone to see if I've

been summoned yet to the downsizing talk, but my mind quickly slips back to the call to the doctor's office. I check to see if they called while I had my phone on silent.

No, not yet. Why can't they call me back? Surely they know by now that my grandmother isn't in her right mind and needs medication.

I don't have time to obsess about her. Grammy will be fine. Surely the doctor will figure it out.

But how? You can't drop a car off at a mechanic's and not tell him what's wrong with it, and hope he'll figure out that it makes a squealing noise whenever you put it in reverse. What if he never tries putting it in reverse?

What if Grammy seems lucid for the five minutes the doctor talks to her and he considers her fine? Then we'll have to go back again.

My desk phone buzzes, and I push the button. "Yes?"

"The partners are asking for you," Nora, my assistant, says.

"Already?"

"Yes."

"Like now?"

"That's what they said. Mr. Southerby's office."

What does it mean that I'm one of the first? I straighten my skirt and try to tame my hair, but it's useless.

I'm just outside Southerby's office door when my phone chirps. I glance down and see that it's the doctor's office. I start to answer, but the secretary sees me and, avoiding eye contact, picks up the phone and tells her boss that I'm here.

I can't take the call now. I'll have to call the doctor back and go through the whole thing again. I drop the phone into my pocket, plaster on my most-reliable-and-committed-employee-who-loves-long-hours smile, and step into the lions' den.

CHAPTER 3

Finn

The old woman is like a parasite, clinging to my brain no matter what else I try to think about. As I deliver a group of five people to a hotel—five people who've squeezed in even though I tried to tell them to take the van behind me—I check my watch. Two hours since Callie's appointment. She hasn't called me to come get her.

Is she okay?

Disgusted with myself for worrying about her, I turn and head back to the hospital. I pull up in the drive-through area and leave my car running again while I retrace my steps to the waiting area and look around for the old woman.

There she sits, exactly where I left her. Her chin has dropped to her chest, and she's sound asleep. "You gotta be kidding me." I storm toward the disinterested receptionist and step in front of the person she's disinterested in now.

"Excuse me. Has Callie Beecher seen the doctor yet?"

She looks just past me. "Sir, please get in line."

"No," I say, almost yelling. "Come on, just look. She's a hundred and fifty years old and she's been sitting there for two hours. Did Callie Beecher see the doctor or not?"

Too bored for words, the woman types Callie's name into the computer. Her lids lower, and she looks back at me. "It says she wasn't here when they called her."

"What do you mean she wasn't here? Since two o'clock she's been right there where I parked her! I told you they had to go to her, that she might be asleep or hard of hearing."

"I'm sorry, sir, but it's not our job to—"

"To what? Take care of sick people?"

She purses her lips and shoots me a piercing look.

"So you're telling me that she hasn't seen him? Then take her back now. I'll wait."

"It doesn't work that way, sir. I'm helping this gentleman right now. Please get in line."

I slap both hands on the counter. "Take her back now, or I'm going to make the rest of your day a living nightmare!"

The woman rises to her feet as someone else—a manager?—comes around the wall. "What's going on here?"

The receptionist turns away from me and whispers something to the manager, and they both look back at me like I'm a security risk. "Okay," the manager says to me. "Bring her on in."

"Oh no," I say quickly. "I'm not bringing her in. I'm not a family member. I don't want to see the doctor with her. I'm just her ride." I point to her. "You have to go over there and get her. She can't be the first old person in a wheelchair who's ever come here. What *are* you people?"

The manager looks frazzled and goes toward Callie, roughly slaps her footrests up, and unlocks the chair. The nurse with the thighs comes to the door to call someone else, but the manager shoves Callie toward her. Callie's head bobs.

"She needs to see Dr. Patrick right away," the manager tells the nurse. "Otherwise this gentleman here who isn't a family member and won't lift a finger is going to pitch a holy fit, and we'll have to call security."

"I'm the cab driver," I grit out.

Callie comes awake as the nurse rolls her through the door, and I hear her saying, "Where are my manners?"

Blowing out an irritated breath, I drop into a chair and pick up a women's magazine that lies on the seat next to me. I flip to the back where they usually keep recipes. I pause at a picture of beef bourguignon and read over the ingredients. Red onions? Who puts red onions in beef bourguignon? Everyone knows you make it with pearl onions.

Amateurs.

I flip through the other recipes and conclude that no one on the magazine staff has tested any of these dishes, otherwise they'd know better.

My culinary teacher would have gotten a good laugh out of this.

I fling the magazine into a chair a couple of seats away and cross my arms. My leg jitters as thoughts flit through my mind about what a fool I was to come back here and sign up for this. I could have just waited and let her genius family—wherever they are—look for her and realize that sending her to the doctor on her own was a bad idea. It's not my job to watch over her.

There's a TV on in the upper corner of the room and I try to watch it, but it's a soap opera, and anyway, the sound is off. I think of asking if they can change the channel to a sports network and crank up the sound a little, but the receptionist still glares at me every time our eyes meet.

Incompetent.

Callie probably won't be back here for a while, so I go to move my still-running cab to a parking space. While I'm in the car, I radio LuAnn. "Listen, this two-hundred-year-old woman you sent me to drive this morning? I'm having to wait for her at the hospital because she isn't in her right mind and probably can't call me to save her life."

"But I was about to give you another fare."

"Can't do it. It's a long story. Listen, did she

call this in herself, or did someone else book the cab?"

"I think somebody else did. A woman, I think."

"Did she leave her name or phone number?"

"No. Why?"

"I'm just thinking she needs to understand that this lady can't do this alone. I don't know what anyone is thinking to send her off with a cab driver when she can't hold a thought for more than two seconds."

"Sounds bad. You're a good man, Finn."

"Shut up," I say and click off the phone. Sometimes I hate LuAnn.

I lock my cab and go back in. She still hasn't reemerged. I sit down, shaking my head at my own stupidity in waiting for her. I'm losing money by the minute.

Rubbing my jaw, I mentally add the amount in my head. I need that money, since it's almost the end of the month. It isn't likely she's a tipper. I'll be lucky if she pays me at all, and what am I going to do about that? Wrestle her purse out of her arthritic grip and pull out her wallet?

Yeah, that isn't going to happen.

The door to the examining room opens, and I

see Callie being wheeled out by a more pleasant-looking nurse whose thighs haven't been maligned. But there could be other slights I don't know about, because Callie is chatting her up.

I step toward her.

"Sir, the doctor would like to speak to you, if you could come back."

"No, no way. I'm not her son. I'm her cab driver."

"Oh, I'm sorry. Well, the doctor needs to speak to her family. And she has a prescription that was called into Walgreens."

I groan. "Walgreens?"

"Yes. The one closest to her address. She needs it. Can you get it for her?"

My temples are so tight I can feel my veins protruding. "I guess so."

Callie says a heartfelt good-bye to the woman, then looks up at me as I push her out the door. "I'm Finn, the cab driver," I say before she can ask me. "How are you, ma'am?"

"Have I eaten today?" she asks. "My stomach feels a little queasy."

Wonderful. Now I'll have to feed her.

I get her into the cab and hit the drive-through

lane at Walgreens. Thankfully, there isn't much of a wait. There's no charge for the meds, which must mean her insurance covers it. At least I don't have to put that on her tab. I keep the meter running, but something tells me it won't matter. It isn't like I'm going to be paid.

When we have the prescription—which is covered by her insurance—I reach over the back seat to hand her the bag, but she's nodded off again. I raise up, lean over the seat, and stuff it into her purse without looking at it. The medication is none of my business.

I drive Callie back to her house and wake her gently, then get her into her wheelchair. She manages to dig out her keys, so I wheel her to the door. As we go in, she looks around like she doesn't recognize the place.

"Ma'am, can I get you anything before I leave?" I ask.

She looks up at me. "No, thank you."

"I could . . . I'll get you something to eat."

"No, that's all right," she says.

"You have to eat. You were there for hours and it's dinnertime, and I don't know if you had lunch."

"You're a sweet boy," she says.

A knot forms in my throat as I go into her kitchen and look in the refrigerator. Someone has stocked it with a few dishes of Tupperware. I pull out one and open it, take a whiff. It's a casserole, and it actually smells recent. I spoon it into a bowl and nuke it.

I set the table, then go get her and roll her chair up to it. She has a pleasant look on her face as I do, as though she enjoys being pampered, even if she doesn't have a clue who's doing it. For all she knows I'm an ax murderer warming up her food before I decapitate her. I get the food out and check to see if it's too hot.

"Do you know who made this?" I ask as I put it in front of her.

"Made what?"

"The casserole. That you're eating."

"It's very tasty," she says. "Thank you so much."

Sighing, I go to the TV and turn it on so she can see it. It's already turned up to bullhorn level.

"Okay, I'll be going now. If you'd like me to get you your purse, you could just . . . pay me."

She looks confused. "Pay you?"

"I'm the cab driver," I repeat for the five thousandth time.

"Of course. Yes. How much do I owe you?"

"Forty-three dollars," I say weakly. "That includes the trip to the drugstore."

She's looking around, so I get her purse and hand it to her. She digs out her checkbook and a pen. She's going to write me a check? I want to tell her I don't take checks, but it doesn't seem worth it. I'll just take it and get out of here.

As she hands me the check, I point out the bag I've stuffed into her purse. "Don't forget your medication."

"My what?"

I sigh again and snatch the paper sack out of her purse, pull the bottle out. "It says to take it three times a day with food." I open it and shake one into my hand, get her some water in a glass, and hand it to her. "Take this."

She does as she's told.

"Okay, I've got to go now." I jot a note onto a Post-it pad beside her wall phone, telling whoever cares for her to call the doctor. I add that she's had one dose of medication. I leave a business card next to it. "Miss Callie, if your family wants to talk to me, they can call me at this number. There is family, isn't there?"

"Of course," she says, beaming.

"Okay, I'm putting it right here." I point to the counter. "Are you going to be okay now?"

"Yes, thank you," she says. "You're such a charming young man."

I almost laugh, but I don't want to get pulled into banter with her. My mother used to say that about me when I was four. I demonstrated that charm in spades when she was dying and I didn't even go to visit.

I suddenly have to get out of here. "Thank you, ma'am. I'm going now."

I try not to look back as I pull her locked door shut behind me and return to my cab.

CHAPTER 4

Sydney

The news is good, or I think it is, until the partners tell me they'll revisit my employment after my ridiculous case is over.

No pressure.

"I'm totally committed to the firm," I tell them. "It's just that . . . I wish this weren't the case I was being judged on. I'd rather be judged on the other work I've done so far, like the Krielig case."

Jacoby speaks in that accent that hits just south of British and just north of Bostonian. He's lived in St. Louis his whole life, so one has to wonder . . .

"There is no unimportant case," he says. "We're

quite aware that the Darco case is challenging, but Steve Darco's father is one of our biggest clients, billing in the millions each year, and as small as this is, it's important. If we were to upset him and lose his business, well . . . all of our jobs would be in jeopardy."

"Yes, of course." I don't mention that it's odd that they didn't assign a single partner to this case since it's so important. But it's probably because none of them wants to become a laughingstock.

Southerby shoves his unlit cigarette into his mouth and talks around it. I wonder if he sucked a pacifier until he was in middle school.

"Meanwhile, you need to absorb some of the cases the other associates are working on after we notify them that they're leaving."

I narrow my eyes. "Can you tell me how many you're letting go?"

"Nope," he says. "You'll know by day's end."

"I'm very committed, Mr. Southerby. I will stay long hours and work weekends, even during the Christmas holidays. You'll see that I have the stamina of ten people." I can see right away from their expressions that I've oversold myself.

"You'll have to," Southerby says. "We all will."

My hands are shaking as I leave the room. I can't regulate the adrenaline surging through my body now. Coffee will make it worse, but I'm so tired that I need it, so I stop by the break room that is a ghost town right now. I guess everyone is trying to look committed as they wait to be called.

As I get back to my office, Joanie rushes in, her arms full of files. "We're still here," she whispers. "I can't believe it. Imagine being let go because you worked second chair to the worst lawyer in the firm and he messed up the case."

"Craig was let go?"

"Yes. They escorted him out. It was brutal."

"Life's not fair."

"No, but right now it seems fair to us. I got the Boliver case and the Hilton case, which is interesting because they both have court dates on the same day. I'll have to get a stay on one of them if I can't get them to settle."

I sip my coffee, though the cup trembles in my hand. "I'm only here until they see how I do on the worst case this firm has ever taken to court."

Joanie covers her mouth and breathes a horrified laugh. "I know it's not funny."

"No, my friend, it is not." My phone vibrates again. "The doctor! I have to take this!" I click it on. "This is Sydney Clifton."

"This is Dr. Patrick," the man says.

"Dr. Patrick! Your voice is the most wonderful sound in the world. I want to kiss you!"

He chuckles. "Well, not what I expected."

"I've been calling about my grandmother, Callie Beecher. I wanted to bring her, but we had a huge meeting at my law firm today in which they told us that they're downsizing some of us, and we've been working like dogs to appear committed, so I sent her in a cab and I don't know if she got there or not, but—"

I guess I'm going on too long, because he interrupts me. "Your grandmother was here."

"She's not herself," I blurt. "I wrote her symptoms on a piece of paper in her purse, but she may have forgotten to give them to you."

"She didn't give them to us, but we observed some of the problems, and we ran some blood work and a few other tests. She has a UTI so I've prescribed her some antibiotics. UTIs do cause confusion sometimes."

"Have you gotten results from any of the other tests yet?"

"Not yet. I'm concerned about some of the other symptoms we're seeing, but I need all the results before I can conclude anything."

I look down at the stack of files, then my gaze drifts toward the glass wall, where the partners have clustered in the hallway and are talking in hushed tones. Joanie has already slipped back out.

"I'll call you when I get the results," he says. "We may need to do more tests."

"Okay, sure. Do you think she'll be all right?"

"We'll talk later, when I know more."

I'm a little disturbed as I hang up, but I have to push it out of my mind. I have to focus on the court case that starts tomorrow. My opening statement isn't finished. What I want to say is that the plaintiff brought a boatload of alcohol to a dorm party, got drunk, then crashed into the BK. End of story.

That probably won't help with my job security. I really need to change my attitude by morning.

CHAPTER 5

Finn

I wake up in the wee hours of morning, covered in sweat. The dream I've just had is of my mother lying in a hospital bed, weighing eighty pounds, with tubes to keep her breathing until I could get there. In the dream, I stepped into the doorway, but that thing—that horrible thing I couldn't escape—came over me, and I backed into the hall and left the building.

The problem with the dream is that it really happened. I'm a coward.

She died that night. She gave up on waiting for me.

It's only two a.m., and I need to sleep. Driving without sleep is miserable, not to mention dangerous, and I have to work today. I have to make my rent money or I'll be evicted right after Christmas.

The robbery a couple of weeks ago—in which some thug pointed a gun at my head and took every dollar I had—really set me back. I haven't made it up yet. Emotionally, it helped a little that they caught the guy a few days later, and I had the privilege of identifying him in a lineup. But the money was long gone.

I turn on the TV, the volume turned down low, and try to sleep in my recliner, but it still evades me. Finally, I give up. It's now five a.m., so I put on a pot of coffee and take a shower.

When I get into my cab and sign in with dispatch, I'm feeling the fatigue.

"I've got a call for you already," LuAnn says in a much too upbeat voice. "They called and asked for you specifically."

"Great." I like repeat customers. "What's the name?"

"Callie Beecher."

I groan. "No! Not her again. I can't afford this!"

"She paid you last night, didn't she?"

"She wrote a check."

"Well, cash it."

"I will, but odds are it'll bounce, meaning I can't pay you your share, meaning I'm wasting all this time. Seriously, I can't drive her again today. Where does she need to go, anyway?"

"She didn't say."

"So did a family member call again?"

"No, she called herself and asked for 'that nice young man.' I thought she was talking about Lamar, but no, it was you. Who knew?"

I brush the hair back off my forehead. "You're killing me."

"I told her you'd come."

"Of course you did."

I drive to Callie's, feeling sorry for myself. If this goes anything like it did yesterday, I'll have to feign a headache and tell her I'll get her a replacement cabbie.

How did she even remember me? She must have gotten the number off my card.

I don't bother to honk my horn. Instead, I cut off my ignition and go right to her door.

"Hello," Callie says through the screen before I can even knock. "Come in, sweet boy."

Surprised, I open the door and step inside. "Ms. Beecher? You called for me?"

"Please, call me Callie."

"Okay, Miss Callie."

She looks much more awake, and she has makeup on. Powder, blush, and a little lipstick. "You look like you're feeling better today," I say. "Where did you want me to take you?"

She seems suddenly confused, and looks around for something.

"Are you looking for your purse?"

"Yes, I think so."

"It's in your lap."

She laughs as though embarrassed, then digs through it.

"You were going to tell me where we're going?"

"Yes, that's right." She pulls out a sheet of paper. "I try to write things down, but then I forget where I put the list. Here . . . this is it."

I take the list and see a bunch of words that have no meaning to me. "Uh . . . there are several things here."

"Yes, I want to hire you for the whole day."

"Ma'am, that would cost a lot of money."

"I'll pay you," she assures me. "Can you take me?"

I hate to say no to a woman who's three hundred years old. "Okay, fine." I do a quick calculation in my head. If I can keep the meter running all day, I can earn enough to pay the rest of my rent. Which means I don't really have the luxury of saying no. I clap my hands together. "Okay, let's go."

I get her out to the car, hook her in, and put her wheelchair in the trunk. "So what's first on the list, ma'am?"

"Macy's Department Store. I have to pick up a few more things for Christmas."

This isn't going to turn out well. She's planning to wheel around the store in her chair when she can't even move herself? I have a bad feeling as I drive the few miles to the mall. I pull in front of the store. "I have to keep the meter running," I say.

"Of course you do. Where are we now?"

"Macy's. Christmas shopping." I get out and get her wheelchair. When I open the back seat and help her into the wheelchair, I ask, "How are you going to get around?"

"Well, I . . . I don't know. I suppose I . . ."

I can't believe this. "See, I don't go in with people and help them shop. I drive. That's it."

She gives me a vacant look.

"I can't keep my meter running if I turn my car off."

She smiles as if she's just noticed me. This isn't going well. "Miss Callie, do you need me to go in with you and push you?"

"Would you mind?" she asks, beaming. "You're such a delightful young man."

"That's me. Delightful. You're going to have to wait here while I find a parking space."

"I won't go anywhere."

"Tell me about it," I mumble under my breath. Biting my bottom lip, I move the cab and turn the car—and the meter—off. How am I going to log these minutes?

Shaking my head, I go back to Callie and roll her into the store.

CHAPTER 6

Sydney

I meet with my client in a tiny interview room adjacent to the courtroom before we're in session this morning. Court starts at eight thirty, and I'd asked him to be here at seven thirty, but he's thirty minutes late. He looks like he has a hangover. His hair is greasy, and he's unshaven and has dark circles under his eyes.

But having already interviewed him several times, I was prepared for this. I hand him a bottle of Pedialyte—which I bought in the baby section of the grocery store. It's for children with dehydration. "Drink this."

He grimaces. "I hate this stuff. Have you ever tasted it?"

"Drink it, Steve. I'm serious." I open the top. "Take the bottle and chug it. It'll rehydrate you and help with your hangover. There's a jury in there, and you'd better not look like you just crawled in from another party."

He takes the bottle and sips, then winces again.

I dig into my bag and pull out some hair-styling gel I bought for this very purpose. "Put this in your hair so it looks like you care."

"I do care. Have you seen this scar on my face? Somebody's got to pay for it."

I want to tell him that he's responsible for the scar on his face, but then he'd call his father, who is in the gallery already, and he'd convince him I'm the wrong lawyer—which I am—and my job will be toast.

"And they will pay. Really, I think this will look good on you. The jurors like people who are well groomed. Oh, and I brought an electric razor. Maybe you should shave."

"So you don't think I'm well groomed?"

Again I bite my tongue, and I don't say that I'm

sure he was well groomed right after the last time he showered. "Drink some more."

"Will I have to say anything today?"

"No. We went over all this. You're not testifying at all."

"Well, if somebody trashes me, I need to defend myself."

"That's my job. Come on. Hair."

He sips some more of the Pedialyte, then squeezes a big glob of gel into his hair and sweeps it back with his fingers. It looks better. After he's run the razor over his face, he still has the beginning of a beard, but it at least looks deliberate. There are a few young women on the jury—I made sure of it. They might like the look.

He does have on a starched shirt, which I'm sure his mother arranged for. "Tuck the shirt in. You have a belt?"

He grins. "You have one of those, too?"

"No, I didn't bring one."

He makes a *sheesh*ing noise like he's messing with me. "Yes. I have one on. But why do I have to tuck it? Even my professors don't tuck their shirts in."

"There are some middle-aged people on the jury. You're doing it for them."

I can't believe his dad didn't make him tuck it in already, but it's clear that this kid calls the shots in his family and everyone falls into line. The man who runs a Fortune 500 company with thousands of employees can't make his son tuck his shirt in.

It'll take all my wits to keep the jury from sensing that.

He finally tucks it in, and he looks presentable. I've chosen not to put him in a suit and tie because I want him to look young and innocent. This might work if I can keep him from showing his true colors.

CHAPTER 7

Finn

"That young man is going to cheat on his wife."

Callie's loud proclamation embarrasses me, but she isn't speaking to me. She's talking to the Macy's salesclerk who's helping her.

The girl seems amused. "Why do you think so?"

"Because she's let herself go. Look at her! He's a nice-looking man, and she hasn't even washed her hair."

The woman with the greasy hair hears her and looks over, indignant. I step away from the wheelchair and pick up some towels as if I'm examining the thread count. The woman storms off, her husband trailing innocently behind her.

The Christmas music piping over the speakers is too loud, playing some ridiculous version of "Deck the Halls." Why can't people just leave a good melody alone?

"And those pants they wear are very unattractive," Callie says. "Why would anyone want to wear elastic pants that show every dimple?"

The clerk signals her coworker to get her to listen in. "They're yoga pants."

"It's like wearing your leotard out in public."

I step forward. "Are we finished here?"

Callie looks up at me like she doesn't recognize me.

"Finn, the cab driver," I say, and that smile takes over her face again. "Shouldn't we go? We have other things on the list."

"The list?" Callie asks.

I consider backing off and taking her home, but she'll remember as soon as she sees that list again. It's sticking up out of a pocket in her purse. I point to it. She grabs it and reads it. "A gift for Sydney. Did I get one?"

"You bought something," I say, lifting the bag. "I don't know who it's for. Who's Sydney?"

"My . . . uh . . . What was I saying?"

"Who Sydney is. Your granddaughter?"

"Yes, that's right."

I wonder why Sydney isn't the one taking her to the doctor and going shopping with her. I round a Christmas tree in our path and almost run into another one. How many ways do they really need to remind us of this season?

Just as I'm eyeing the exit, the sound of Christmas carolers singing "O Little Town of Bethlehem" distracts her. She tries to turn in her wheelchair to see them. "Oh, look. Aren't they lovely?"

Groaning, I turn and see that just outside the mall exit of the store, an ensemble of singers dressed in Victorian outfits are launching into a concert. Just my luck.

"Let's go see them!" Callie says, clapping her hands. "Oh, I love the singing!"

I push her through the displays and cross the store to that exit. I park her in front of the singers. She sways in her chair, clapping her skinny hands with the song.

There's a coffee store behind us, so I leave Callie by the singers, hurry in, and order a coffee. I take my time fixing it, then I walk back over to Callie. She sees me coming and stops clapping to reach out for my cup. "Oh, you didn't have to get me that. You're such a sweet boy."

Reluctantly, I surrender the coffee and wonder if I should take the time to go back and get another one. But the singers end their little concert.

"Ready to go now?" I ask her.

She looks at me, confused. "I don't know where my head is," she says. "What did I buy?"

I open the bag and show her.

She looks disappointed. "Towels aren't a good gift for her."

"You bought them."

"That won't do. I have to get her something else. What's a good gift?"

It took her a half hour to find and buy the towels. Now she doesn't want them? What am I supposed to do? Take them back before we've even left the store?

"I don't know anything about her," I say. "But everyone needs towels."

"She deserves something special."

"Something special in this store, I hope. And if you make me help you pick out clothes, I'm going to hurl myself into the elevator shaft."

"What, dear?"

"Nothing."

I wheel her around the home section, to the jewelry, the shoes, the purses. She doesn't buy anything. I don't even know if she's still lucid.

Finally, I convince her to go to the next place on her list. The towels will have to do. It isn't like this Sydney person will hold it against her thousand-year-old grandmother if she doesn't get her something she wants.

Truth be told, this revered granddaughter doesn't deserve anything, or Callie wouldn't be with some random cab driver for the second day in a row.

I get Callie out of the store and back to the cab. She's waning by the time we reach the car. I wonder if she's had breakfast.

CHAPTER 8

Finn

Just what I need. Callie has fallen asleep in my back seat, and I have no idea where she wanted to go next.

This is ridiculous. Even indulging in this fantasy of hers—that she can hire me all day to trot her all over town to buy gifts for people who may or may not even exist—is insane. I have to end it right now.

I go around the block and head back to her house. I'm the one who needs to sleep. And so much for the rent money. Not only am I not going to get the day's pay, I won't even make what I usually do because I've been off the meter for half the morning.

Life always turns out this way for me. Some people are given lemons and they make lemonade—and frankly, I detest those people—and some, like me, are given acorns, and unless you're a squirrel or a *Naked and Afraid* contestant, they are pretty much useless.

I reach Callie's house and pull into the driveway. I look into the back seat. She's still sleeping, her head back and her mouth hanging open. She's going to get a neck cramp.

Sighing, I turn off the meter. "Miss Callie?"

No response. I try again. Still nothing. She doesn't even flinch.

Her face looks pale, and it occurs to me that she might be . . . No, she wouldn't dare die in my back seat! I jump out, open the back door, and lean in. I shake her. "Miss Callie?"

She stirs then, and I blow out a sigh of relief. "Miss Callie? Wake up. We're here."

Her eyes come open, and she looks around, confused. Then she smiles up at me.

"We're at your house. I'll get your wheelchair." I get her chair, and when I'm back at her door, she's digging through her purse. I don't know if she's thinking about paying me, but I highly doubt it. But while she's in there, I might as well try.

"Ma'am, that fare is twenty-two dollars. Eleven for taking you to the mall, and another eleven to come back." I should add on the time in between spent walking around Macy's, but it would be too complicated to explain to her.

"Oh yes," she says, pulling out an oversize wallet. She opens the coin purse and digs through, pulling out a few quarters.

"No, ma'am. It's twenty-two *dollars*. I doubt you have all that in change."

She looks embarrassed and opens the billfold part. She pulls out two twenties and hands them to me. "I don't have change."

"I'll get it," I tell her.

She grabs my hand. "It's all right, sweet boy. You keep it. Buy something nice."

Like shelter? I want to say. "Thank you, ma'am."

I help her out. She leans on me as I maneuver her into the wheelchair. I wheel her up to her door. "Your key?"

"Oh yes." She plunges into her nightmare of a purse again, and I cringe at the sound of useless items rattling against each other. "I'm afraid I can't find it," she says finally. "It's not in here."

Dread twists in my gut again. "May I look?"

She looks a little suspicious, but I don't care. I pull her purse open as wide as I can get it and look past the wallet and checkbook, the hairbrush and lipsticks.

There are no keys. "Are you kidding me?" I mutter. "Seriously? You came away without your keys?" I open the screen door and try the doorknob, but it's locked. I locked it myself. Why didn't I check to make sure she had her key?

"Miss Callie, are you sure you don't have keys in a pocket somewhere? Maybe you dropped them into your shopping bag?" I grab the bag hanging on the handle of the chair and look into it. Nope.

I'm ready to kick something, but I don't want to frighten her into a heart attack. What am I going to do now?

She's distracted by the weeds in her garden now, as if she's already forgotten that she lost her key.

"Miss Callie, do you have your granddaughter's phone number anywhere?"

"What? Oh yes. Somewhere."

"How do you get in touch with her when you need her?"

"In touch with who?"

"Your granddaughter. What's her name again? Sydney?"

"Yes, Sydney."

"I need a phone number."

The distressed look on Callie's face makes me regret my harsh tone. She can't help this. It isn't her fault. It's LuAnn's. She should have sent Lamar instead of putting me through this again. I'm going to get ulcers.

This isn't accomplishing anything. She doesn't know where her keys are, we're locked out, and Sydney is a world away since I don't know her last name and have no way of finding her.

I turn Callie's chair around and push her back toward the cab.

"Where are we going?" she asks.

"I would love to know that myself." I help her back into the cab and roughly collapse the chair again. "Somebody is going to have to pay for this," I mutter. "This is my work. I don't do it for my health. I do it to put a roof over my head."

She doesn't seem to hear me. I put the chair back in the trunk. Acorns. Once again, I'm stuck with acorns instead of lemons. Congratulations to all those who get lemons. You could make lemonade out of that, and lemon icebox pie, and lemon bars, and lemon chicken. You could season with it and add it to other dishes. You could use the juice on fish and steak.

But acorns . . .

I back out of the driveway and start my meter running again.

CHAPTER 9

Sydney

The college culture today is not about education," I say to the jury. They look alert and interested in the handsome boy behind the plaintiff's table. "It's not about career training. It's not about learning. It's not about starting the path to your future. Instead, it's about drinking and partying and frat hazings and hookups. College has taught these kids that they're entitled, and that it's all about having fun instead of preparing for a productive life. And my client, Steve Darco, is a victim of that culture."

The jury seems locked into what I'm saying. I stayed at the office most of the night, practicing this opening statement. I had no desire to go back to the office after getting Grammy into bed, but I knew I had to so the partners would hear about my commitment. I didn't get home until two a.m.

I wonder if I should even keep my house. Maybe I just need to move in with her.

"Yes, I'm sure Mr. Renzo will call him a partier. He's eighteen. His father and mother sent him to college, trusting that he would be taken care of on campus. Trusting that the university could protect him. But they didn't."

The words couldn't be further from what I really believe. I don't like victimhood, and I hate excuses, and I know the college isn't any more responsible for his behavior than the Burger King is. But I have a job to do, and that is to keep this kid from shouldering the blame.

When I'm finished, I take my seat next to Steve. He grins and punches a fist at me, as if I'm going to fist bump him right in front of the jury. I look down at my notes and pretend I didn't see it.

God, help me.

The attorney for the college gets up and starts his completely logical spiel, expressing everything I really think.

"Do you remember the lady who sued McDonald's because her coffee was too hot?" he asks the jury. "This case is just that ludicrous. Young Mr. Darco brings two kegs to the third floor of the Jameson dorm, and a thousand dollars' worth of liquor, breaking the school's rules." He goes back to his table as he speaks, and picks up a sheet of paper. "This is the form he signed before moving in, where this rule is spelled out. Then he leaves the campus, drunk, in his car, and crashes the vehicle into the Burger King, and we're supposed to agree that the university is liable for this? Are you kidding me?"

I sigh and Steve whispers, "Dude, that's harsh." He looks back at his parents sitting behind us, as if his dad will stand up and tell the attorney to pipe down.

I don't let myself roll my eyes.

"Can't you object?" he whispers. "The whole BK thing is a separate act."

I shake my head. "It's the event we're accusing the college of causing." I hate myself for saying those words.

"They did cause it," Steve says.

I wish I could go home and take a nap. It's going to be a long day.

CHAPTER 10

Finn

I'm stuck with Callie. What am I supposed to do? Move the woman into my apartment if we can't get in touch with her AWOL granddaughter? If I have to break a window to get her inside her house before day's end, I will.

But right now, I have to deal with it. I'm sure Callie hasn't eaten, so I'll have to feed her. And what about her medication? Is it in her purse? Does she need any now?

Where can I take her? I don't even know if someone her age would eat something from Arby's or McDonald's. This is going to be a long, drawn-out thing, and I won't be able to keep my meter running. This day is just getting better and better.

I try to think where someone like Callie might eat. My mother used to go to Lulu's a lot. It's a cafeteria-style joint that old people love. There's one not far from here. I drive there and pull into the parking lot, but when I try to get Callie out, she's sleeping so deeply that I hate to wake her.

Her list is peeking out of the top of her purse, so I pull it out. She's written, "Dry Cleaners, Bank," and some things that don't register with me.

Was she even in her right mind when she wrote the list? I groan and sit down on the back seat next to her. I peek into her purse again, careful not to stick my hands in it. You don't stick your hands in a woman's purse, I learned long ago. They have stuff in it they don't want you to see. Primping tools and breath mints and wadded receipts, makeup and hairbrushes and big fat wallets, bricks and whatnot. There's no telling what someone her age has in that thing. It could be forty years of accumulated detritus.

I see two medicine bottles crammed at the top. I glance up, making sure she's sleeping soundly enough that she won't spring awake the second I pull them out. Wincing, I reach in without looking—as if turning my head makes my invasion of her private things okay—and I grab the bottles. I pull them out and read the labels.

Great. Just as I feared, it's time for one of them. I've never heard of this medication, but she clearly needs it. The bottle says to take it with food. I'll have to wake her up.

I take my time getting her wheelchair, then lean in and shake her. "Miss Callie?"

She stirs but doesn't wake. "Lady, I need you to wake up."

Her eyes flutter open, and she looks up at me, blank.

"We're at the restaurant," I say. "You have medication to take, but you have to have food with it. So come on. I'll take you in."

"Oh yes. Thank you." She's polite even when she's a pain in the neck. I help her out and get her into the wheelchair, reach back in for her purse and set it in her lap. I drop her medications in my pocket so I won't have to go into her purse again.

She perks up as I wheel her in and search for

the least sticky table in the place. There's a sad Christmas tree near the door that has probably absorbed a layer of grease from the food in the cafeteria lines. The ornaments are dusty. They can't do better than that?

Now what? Do I have to take her through the line and find out what she likes? This could take forever.

But Callie is pretty easy. She quickly identifies roast, black-eyed peas, and green beans as all she wants. I get her a roll for good measure, then serve my own plate. I take the plates to the table, then come back to wheel her.

"Thank you, Jesus," she says in a soft voice before she takes her first bite.

"Ma'am, I'm not Jesus. I'm Finn Parrish."

She laughs then as if I've done a great comedy bit. "No, no, sweet boy. I was praying."

I grin. "Oh. Sorry. You didn't have your eyes closed."

"I didn't need my eyes closed," she says. "I can talk to him anytime."

"I bet you can," I mutter under my breath. "Um . . . you have some medications to take." I show them to her. "This one has to be taken now. The other one . . . it says twice a day, so I'm assuming that you took one this morning. Did you?"

"Yes, I'm sure I did."

I'm pretty sure she's just guessing. "Okay." I open the one she needs now and pour it into her hand. I watch her swallow it, then I drop the bottles back into her purse.

"You're a nice young man," she says. "Are you married?"

Is she coming on to me? "No, ma'am. I'm not."

"Because I have a beautiful granddaughter."

"Yeah, about her. Have you remembered how we can reach her? Sydney, isn't it?"

"You know her? She hasn't mentioned you."

I doubt that, at this moment, Callie has any inkling who I am. I could be Sydney's husband for all she knows. "No, I haven't met her. But I'd really like to. Do you have her number in that lovely head of yours?"

She laughs again and shakes her finger, as if this time *I've* flirted with *her*. "You're a flatterer, aren't you?"

"Sydney's phone number?" I ask. "Do you have it? Or even her last name?"

Her smile fades, and she looks confused. "Oh my, I don't know where my head is. I know, but I can't think of it right now."

That's progress. At least she knows she's forgetting. "Keep trying," I say. "I can't take you home until you think of it because you're locked out of your house."

"Yes," she says. "I'll try."

She's stopped eating, so I point to the food again. "Food looks good. Don't you want more?"

"Yes," she says, suddenly remembering it. "It's good, but not as good as my own cooking."

"You cook?" I ask. "I used to cook."

"Used to?"

"Yeah. Had a restaurant. It went under, so . . . now I'm driving a cab."

"What did you cook?"

I look at her, perplexed. Has she suddenly grown lucid? Is her medication working that quickly, or is her dementia a come-and-go kind of thing? "French haute cuisine. I studied in Paris at Le Cordon Bleu."

"Paris?" she asks, delighted. "That's fascinating. I went to Paris once. My husband took me there for our anniversary. Oh, the food!" Her eyes mist over, and I can see that it's a sweet memory. "Your mother must have been so very proud."

"Uh . . . yeah. She was." The thought flattens my appetite. The truth is that she never had much opportunity to tell me how proud she was, because I didn't go home that much after Paris. I shove my plate away. "So . . . you seem to be feeling better. Let's talk about Sydney again."

"Sydney," she says, and her smile brightens even more. "She's such a lovely girl. And so smart."

"I bet. She probably has a great personality too, huh?"

"Everyone likes Sydney. She's a blonde, you know. Taller than me. She must get the height from her father, because she sure didn't get it from our side of the family. She could be a model, but she decided to go to that other school. That . . . what do they call it?"

"No clue," I say. "So . . . remembering her last name yet? Her number? Maybe an address or where she works?"

Again that distressed look comes over her.

"I'd love to meet her," I say again.

She pokes through her purse but seems to forget

what she's looking for. "I don't know what I was thinking."

"Sydney," I prompt.

She finds her list and pulls it out. "Oh, I need to run these errands. I have so much to do."

Oh boy. I rub my face. "Yeah. You said that before you fell asleep in my cab." *Before I had to feed and medicate you.*

"All right," I say, getting up. "If you've eaten all you want, we can go. Unless you want dessert."

"No, I'm fine, thank you."

I get her back to my car and start the meter running again. "So you want to go to a dry cleaners? Which one?"

"The one near my house."

Great. Well, at least I'm driving again, which means the meter is on, so I'm at least getting paid. I drive toward her house and spot a dry cleaner's just before I get to her street. "Is this it?"

She's zoned out, looking on the wrong side of the car. I snap my fingers. "Miss Callie? The dry cleaners?"

"Yes, that's the one."

I pull into the parking lot. "I could run in and get your clothes for you. You could wait here."

"No, no, I need to go in. I have to talk to that nice young man in there."

Perfect.

I get her chair out. This is getting old. It pains me to turn off the meter again, but how long can it take to pick up dry cleaning?

CHAPTER 11

Sydney

After a grueling lunch with Steve in the interview room during the midday recess, I squeeze in a phone call to Grammy's house phone. It goes straight to voice mail again—a voice mail box that has never been set up or checked. I try the cell phone I gave her, but I didn't charge it last night, and she never remembers to take it with her, anyway. It goes straight to voice mail, too. Where is she?

I have to remind her that it's time to take her medication again, but now I wonder if something has happened to her. What if she's lying on the floor of the bathroom, yelling, "I've fallen and I can't get up!" like that woman on the commercial? What if she's lapsed into confusion again and doesn't even remember how to answer the phone?

I have to go over there. I check my watch. I only have forty-five minutes left before I have to be back in court. I grab my bag and head for the elevator, wishing I had on different shoes. The men in the office expect the women to dress in heels every day—because everyone knows that a woman only looks professional if she walks on her toes and arches her back until her disks pop.

"You're not leaving, are you?" Steve says behind me.

I punch the down button and look over my shoulder at him. "I have to run to my car for a minute. I'll meet you back in court. Stay in this building. Don't go anywhere."

I ride the elevator down, wishing it would go faster. On the ground floor, I trot out to the parking garage. My parking space is so far away that by the time I get to my car, I have a blister on the side of my foot.

These stupid shoes! Why did I wear them? Why do I even own them?

I accelerate out of the garage and speed to my grandmother's house. The door is closed and locked, which is odd. The first thing Grammy does each day is open that door to "let the air in," even if it's thirty degrees outside. I left it open when I left there this morning after dressing her, and she seemed relatively fine—even better than she has in the past few days. The medication is helping her already.

I open the screen and knock on the door, but no one comes, so I use my key to unlock the door. My heartbeat escalates as I step in and look around. "Grammy? Where are you?"

When there's no answer, I kick off my shoes and dash from room to room, certain I'll find her on the floor. Her scooter is here, but she isn't, and neither is her wheelchair or her purse.

Where in the world has she gone?

I pace from room to room, looking for a clue and hoping she'll come back. Her medication isn't here, and the only dish in the sink is the one I left here myself after I made her eat eggs this morning.

So Meals on Wheels hasn't delivered her lunch?

I wait as long as I can, and Grammy still doesn't come back. I can't be late for court.

Finally, I have to leave. I put my dreaded shoes back on, lock the door, and trot to my car.

I make it back just as the judge makes his entrance. I hope no one sees that I'm sweating in December as I hurry to my seat.

CHAPTER 12

Finn

I roll Callie into the dry cleaners and stop at the counter, where the clerks are helping two people in front of us. Callie points to the area behind the counter. "Push me back there."

I frown. "Behind the counter? Ma'am, I don't think you should go there. That's for employees."

"But I need to see him."

She leans forward as if trying to get up, but I touch her shoulder. "Okay, stay in the chair, ma'am. I'll take you." I catch a clerk's eye as I push her toward the gap in the counter. "Is it okay if she goes back there?"

"Sure. Hi, Mrs. Beecher. How are you today?"

Callie gushes all over the girl. She must have done this before. I push her behind the counter, past several green bags full of clothes, to the door that has the Manager sign on it.

I knock.

"Come in," a man calls.

I open the door and lean in. "Sorry to bother you. Callie Beecher insists on talking to you. I don't know if you shrank her best sweater or didn't get out a stain, but she's pretty set on seeing you face-to-face."

He gets up and comes around his desk, smiling. "Mrs. Beecher. My favorite customer. How are you, sweetie?"

Callie beams up at me. "Isn't he handsome?" She winks, and I'm even more embarrassed.

"Yeah, a real prince."

"Give us a minute alone, will you?" she asks.

The man probably feels trapped, but better him than me. I step out of the room and go back around the counter. There's a folding chair by the door, so I sit down. Another Christmas tree blocks the window. What is it with all these trees? There must be no more than thirty square feet of space in this room, and this tree fills up a huge part of it. Hasn't anyone ever heard of decorating with tinsel or something that doesn't impede customer movement?

I can hear laughter through the door. Callie hasn't seemed like a cougar before now, but I wonder if this is a hundred-year-old's idea of flirtation. After a few minutes, the door opens again, and the man wheels her out. "I really appreciate the invitation," he says in a loud voice to accommodate her hearing. "But I've got plans with my family on Christmas. My mother would kill me if I didn't show up."

"Well, that just breaks my heart," Callie says.

"Maybe another time?"

"It has to be on Christmas."

"I'm sorry, Mrs. Beecher. You know I'd do anything for you if I could."

She draws in a heavy breath and lets it out in a rush. "Okay, then."

She's quiet as I get her back into my still-idling car. When I get behind the wheel, I ask, "You okay, Miss Callie?"

"Yes, I guess I am," she says, her voice heavy with disappointment.

I try to think of something to comfort her, but what can I say? There are other fish in the sea? Isn't it a little absurd that I'd be comforting her for unrequited love when she's probably fifty years older than the object of her affections?

"Were you inviting him over for Christmas dinner?"

She doesn't answer, so I glance in the rearview mirror and see her staring out the window. Has she zoned out again?

Finally, she says, "He isn't the right one."

"There'll be others," I say.

Instead of comforting her, my words clearly upset her. Tears redden her eyes.

"You okay?" I ask.

"I'm running out of time," she says.

I'm not sure if she's talking about Christmas. The words sober me, but when she asks me to take her to the bank, I shake my thoughts away. When we get there, I ask, "Do you want to do the drive-through?"

"The what?" she asks.

"The drive-through, where you can do your banking through the . . . Never mind. Guess we're going in."

Once again I consider whether I can leave the car and meter running here, but it doesn't seem like a great idea. It pains me to cut it off, but again I add the amount to the list I'm keeping on my phone.

I get her wheelchair out for the thousandth time today and help her back into it. Inside, I hesitate at the first desk, where a young woman looks up and offers to help us.

"No, thank you," Callie says. "But you're very pretty. Isn't she pretty?" she asks me with a smile.

I can't believe she would put me on the spot this way. "Yes, very pretty."

The employee beams at me. "Thank you."

"Over there, sweet boy," Callie says, pointing to a glass office where a man is working.

I push her to the doorway of the office, and the man looks up. "Well, Mrs. Beecher. We've missed you! How are you?"

He hugs Callie, then reaches to shake my hand. I take it but say, "Cab driver."

"You can wait out there," Callie tells me in a

sweet voice. "I want to talk to this nice young man for a moment."

"Of course." I step back out, closing the door behind me. Good grief. Is she hitting on another man? This is reaching the absurd.

I take a seat and watch through the door as she talks to the man. They're both smiling. Callie looks through her purse, but she clearly can't find what she's looking for.

This doesn't add up. Callie isn't the kind of woman to be flirting with younger men, is she? Maybe in her dementia she thinks she's twenty-two.

She couldn't remember where her keys were, but she remembered where these men worked? Yes, there are notations on her list that probably prompted her memory, but why would this be important enough to have written down while she forgets the location of her keys?

Frustration waxes through me. I check my watch.

After a few minutes, the man gets up and hugs her again, then turns her wheelchair around. I go to the door. As it opens, I hear the man saying, "I'm sure she's lovely. But my girlfriend wouldn't like it."

"You can't make an exception for an old lady?" Callie cajoles.

"Sorry, Mrs. Beecher. But I do appreciate it."

When I have her back in the car, I have to ask again. "So who were you talking about to him? The person he said was probably lovely?"

"My Sydney," she says. "I'm starting to think I have as bad taste in men as she does."

"Sydney has bad taste in men?"

"That's right. Such a sweet girl. She deserves so much."

I seize the opportunity. "So . . . what's Sydney's last name?" I glance back hopefully and see that Callie is faltering. She still can't think of it.

"What about a picture?" I ask. "Do you have a picture of her?" Maybe that will prompt a clue about how to reach her.

When she doesn't answer, I say, "What does Sydney do?"

"She's one of those . . . you know . . . Oh, I can't think of it."

Not helpful. Irritation floods through me again. What am I going to do with Callie?

I look in the rearview mirror and see that she

has drifted off to sleep again, this time with her head at a weird angle. She's probably going to hurt when she wakes up. I pull over and get out, lean into the back seat, straighten her head, and lay it back on the seat.

She never stirs.

Though it's against my better judgment, I take her purse. I'm going in. I have to find her keys or something about Sydney . . . anything that will help me get Callie into her house. I pull out her big wallet, unzip it, and look inside for a key. Nothing. No cash, no key. I move her checkbook, her glasses case . . . then I look in the pocket on the outside of her purse.

Not a key . . . but a cell phone.

"Are you kidding me?" I whisper as I take it out. All along she's had a cell phone in here, probably with her granddaughter's contact info on it, and she hasn't told me? How many times has she dug through that purse today?

I try to turn on the phone. Perfect. The battery is dead. I have to get it juiced up so I can see what's on there.

The phone is different from mine, but I know

what kind of connector it needs. I drive to a drugstore and leave her in the car with the engine idling while I go in. I grab the connector off the carousel that holds the cellular accessories and glance out the window at my car. Did I lock it? What if Callie wakes up and climbs over the seat and drives away?

I chuckle at the thought. And if someone steals it, *they'll* have to deal with Callie, and I'll be off the hook.

But no one steals it, and Callie doesn't go into car-jack mode. She's still there, sleeping deeply, as I get back in. I plug the car charger into my lighter slot and the lightning end into her phone. Then I start driving to nowhere, waiting for it to gain enough power to turn on.

I've driven a few miles when the phone starts up. I pull over into a Jiffy Lube parking lot. There's no passcode on her phone, so I thumb through to her contacts list. On the search bar, I punch in the name *Sydney*. Up comes the name *Sydney Batson*, with a phone number.

Finally! I click the little phone icon next to the number and listen as Sydney's phone rings. I'll tell her to get to her grandmother's house and open the door immediately or I'll dump Grandma on the curb. I would never do that, of course, but she won't know that.

But the phone rings through to voice mail. I want to scream. I leave a message that I have her grandmother and need for her to call me. I realize as I hang up that it sounds like a ransom call. But maybe it'll light a fire.

I go back to her contacts and find her address. Maybe the girl works at home. I turn the car around and head that way. Callie is still sleeping when I get to the little patio home with a double garage and a tiny courtyard out front, home to wilted flowers that desperately need water. Of course. She takes care of her plants like she takes care of her grandmother.

Well, I'll just sit here with the car and meter running all day if I have to, until the notorious Sydney gets home.

Minutes crawl by. I'm tapping my heel and shaking my knee, and finally I slam my fist on the steering wheel. I can't do this. I can't just sit in someone's driveway for hours.

I call her back and leave another message. "This is Finn Parrish. I'm a cab driver your grandmother hired, and I can't take her home because she locked herself out and can't find the key. I don't know what to do with her. I got your address from her phone and I'm sitting in your driveway, and my meter is still running. I have to make a living. Call me back." I give the number again in case she's too dense to look at her caller ID.

I'll mention dropping Callie off at the curb in my next message if she doesn't call me back. I glance in the rearview mirror and see that Callie's head has dropped to that painful angle again. I get out and prop her better, then get back in front.

Another whole day pretty much wasted, and she doesn't even have cash to pay me again. She could write me another check, but for all I know it won't clear the bank. I haven't had a chance to try to cash the one from yesterday.

Maybe God is punishing me. Maybe this is some cosmic what-goes-around-comes-around sting. I probably deserve it after the way I treated my mother. He's been waiting for the right moment, and this is apparently it.

Now God's stuck me with an elderly woman

who's sick. And there really isn't anything I can do about it.

I look back at Callie again. Does she look cold? I turn up the heater, then shrug off my jacket and put it over her.

Whether from cold or not, there's a pallor to her skin as she sleeps that saddens me beyond words. Callie doesn't look well at all. What if she dies right here? What will I do then?

As irritating as she is, she's a sweet woman. She doesn't deserve to die in a cab in her grand-daughter's driveway. Anger shoots through me. I add Sydney's number to my phone, then get out and call her again while I pace up and down the drive-way, and this time I light into her voice mail. "I just want to know what kind of person refuses to call back when I've told you that your sick, confused, Methuselah-contemporary grandmother is sitting in my cab, locked out of her house. This isn't good for her. She needs to be at home, not running all over town, and now she's so deeply asleep that I'm afraid she might not wake up. So why don't you call me back before I put her out on the curb or drop her off at the police station? Or—here's a thought—go unlock her door so she can go home!"

I almost throw the phone after cutting it off, but instead I kick my tire. I get back into the car, wondering why I chose this profession when my other one failed. I've gone from the scent of coq au vin to gas fumes and body odor.

But truth be told, cab driving has been less of an emotional and physical drain. My restaurant clientele let me down—when the economy tanked, they quit coming. But it didn't really matter. By the time I had to sell the restaurant, I was burned out anyway. I was ready to go.

But there were a million other things I could have done. Why did it have to be this? Why do I have to be stranded here with her?

When Callie's phone rings, I jump. I swipe it on. "Hello?"

"Uh . . . hi, this is Sydney Batson." Her voice is clipped, a little angry. "I didn't get your messages until just now because I've been trying a case in court."

A lawyer. I hate lawyers. But yeah, that's a good excuse.

"Let me speak to my grandmother."

"Can't, she's asleep in my car. So are you going to come get her, or unlock her house? This is tying up my whole day."

"You said you had the meter running. You'll get paid."

"It's not about that. She's not well. She needs to be home."

A car pulls into the driveway behind me as I'm talking, and behind the wheel is a woman with a phone to her ear. Is this Sydney?

She waves. "Yes, it's me," she says. "'Bye."

I get out of the car and wait with my hands on my hips.

Sydney is cuter than I expected. She's not tall like a model, as Callie implied. She's a petite blonde with big brown eyes. She heads toward me. "I didn't know she was going to call you. I got her dressed this morning and made sure she had food. I don't even know how she had your number."

"I gave her a card yesterday after I took her to the doctor. And that's another thing. Why would you send her to the doctor with a cab driver? She didn't hear her name yesterday when they called it. I finally had to force them to take her back."

She opens the back door of the cab and leans in. When she sees how deeply her grandmother is sleeping, she gets back out. "She's sleeping so soundly. I hate to wake her."

"I know the feeling," I say. "So . . . what? You're just going to leave her there?"

"No, of course not." She glances back at Callie. "You've taken care of her. I appreciate it." She closes the door quietly, trying not to disturb Callie. "Look, I'm a first-year associate at my law firm, and yesterday they fired a bunch of us. I'm still there, but it's the worst possible time for me to miss work. I started a case in court today, and as you probably know, you can't just ask the judge for a personal day. Besides, my job is hanging by a thread if I don't win this case . . ."

I roll my eyes. "A key? Do you have a key?"

"I'm just saying that I couldn't take her to the doctor yesterday because of an important staff meeting, but she was sick and I wanted her to go. How has she been today?"

"I'm not her nurse," I say. "Do you have the key or not?"

"She keeps an extra one under her mat."

My mouth drops open. "Are you kidding me?"

"No. Did you check there?"

"No! I didn't think anyone was stupid enough to leave a key under their mat. That's the first place anybody would look."

"Clearly not you!"

"You're blaming me? You need to take better care of her!"

Tears spring to Sydney's eyes, but she makes a valiant effort to hold them back. "I get up at five a.m. every day to get over there because that's when she tries to get up. I get her bathed and dressed, feed her, and make sure she's okay until I can check on her at lunch. Then I come home and feed her again and get her into bed. It's not easy!"

I feel bad now. Maybe she isn't a no-account. I lower my voice. "Maybe you need to hire somebody to stay with her."

"I can't afford it, and neither can she. Until recently she was fine in her own home, but she has just gotten worse and worse . . ." She dabs at her eyes. "Wait. You said she called you today. Did she seem more coherent?"

"A little. She had me running all over the place

doing errands. The dry cleaners, the bank. She even went shopping."

"For what? I do all her grocery shopping."

"For Christmas."

Her eyes brighten. "Really? She remembered that it's almost Christmas? That's a good sign, right? The medicine must have already helped her."

"I guess. How old is she, anyway?"

"Eighty."

"Only eighty? I would have thought . . ." My voice thins out.

"She's been so out of it for the last few days. I'm so relieved that she's doing better. I was thinking maybe she had a brain tumor or Alzheimer's . . . but it wouldn't come on that suddenly, would it? If only the doctor would call me back with the results of her tests."

I can't believe I'm still standing here with her. "Okay, well, I can take her home if you want. Or you could take her."

"Look, I know the whole key-under-the-mat thing is disturbing, but I obviously can't control her, and I knew if she ever got locked out, it would be the first and probably only place she would look for it."

"Uh-huh. Well, she didn't."

"She's a strong-willed woman, and having this . . . dementia, or whatever it is . . . it's only making her more strong-willed."

"Ya think?"

She breathes out a huff and shakes her head. "You don't have to be sarcastic."

It's true, I don't. I get back into the cab and grab my phone. I navigate to the Notes section and find the amounts I've logged. "She owes me seventy-seven dollars for today."

She swallows. "Okay. Let me get my purse."

I feel a little sorry for her as she goes back to her car. It sounds like she's strapped and stressed. I know what that feels like.

By the time she returns, I've made up my mind. "Look, don't worry about it. I have a check she wrote me this morning for yesterday. Does she even have enough in her account for that? Just forget it. You don't have to pay."

"No, I insist. You have to make a living." She opens her wallet and pulls out a twenty. "This is all I have right now."

"I take debit cards, but—"

"Okay, the truth is, I only have forty-two dollars in my account. I'm supposed to get paid tomorrow. Can you wait?"

"Sure, don't worry about it."

"Can you help me get her into my car?"

"Of course." I'm elated to get her off my hands.

I get her chair out of the trunk as Sydney crawls in to wake her grandmother up. "Grammy?"

I wheel the chair to the door, and Sydney hands me back my jacket. "Yours?"

"Yeah. She looked cold."

She smiles up at me, like she sees something that I don't want her to see. "Thank you."

I look away as I shrug it back on.

She shakes her grandmother again and, louder, says, "Grammy, wake up!"

Callie stirs and opens her eyes. "Hello, pretty girl. I must have dozed off."

I watch as Sydney gently gets her out of the car and into the wheelchair, then I help get her into the front seat of Sydney's car.

When I've collapsed the chair again and put it into the back, Sydney rolls her window down. "Thank you for taking care of her."

"Sure, no problem."

I go to my car and watch as the girl backs her car out. Relief floods over me like a drug as I head to the airport to make some actual cash.

CHAPTER 13

Finn

My phone chimes at seven thirty the next morning, waking me out of a REM cycle. I grope for my phone and squint at the readout. LuAnn is the last person I want to talk to. But in the interest of job security, I click the phone on. "It's my day off," I say.

"I know. I hope I didn't wake you up."

"Of course you woke me up. If you'd looked at the logs you'd know that I worked until midnight last night trying to make up for the money I lost driving that lady around all day."

"That's why I'm calling. She called this morning and asked me to get in touch with you again."

"No!" I yell. "No way. Tell her I'm not coming."

"She said she owes you money and wants to pay you."

I sit up in bed, rubbing my eyes. "She said that? Did she sound lucid?"

"Yes, she seemed very nice. She called you 'that sweet boy.' I knew right away who she meant."

"Very funny."

"Seriously, I can call her back and tell her you'd rather not."

"No, that's okay. I need the money."

"I thought so."

"All right, I'll go by there."

I hang up and try to go back to sleep, but it doesn't happen. Finally, I surrender to the day.

An hour later, Callie is back in my car. How does this keep happening? I told her that I was off today, that I'd just come to pick up the money. She gave me a hundred dollars cash—which I suppose Sydney got for her—but before I know it, she's grabbing her purse and declaring that she feels so much better that she hopes to get a lot done today.

She won't take no for an answer. Strong-willed doesn't even begin to cover it. I can't be mean to her—though I wish I could—so I dutifully get her into my back seat.

I radio in to LuAnn and tell her I'm on the clock.

"I thought you were off. You were up till midnight making up for—"

"You're not funny, Lu. I gotta go."

"Well, at least you'll be able to pay your rent."

"'Bye." I hang up and look at Callie in the rearview mirror. She looks brighter today, more awake, and she sounds lucid except for her selective hearing about my day off. "Miss Callie, do you have your key to get back in?"

"Yes, thank you."

"Are you sure? Because yesterday you forgot it."

She chuckles in a coy way. "I hate to admit it, but my memory isn't what it used to be."

"No kidding. Hey, have you ever thought of hiring a driver to just drive you around, Miss Callie? Someone who looks after just you?"

She gives me a beautiful smile. "Well, I did that, didn't I?"

"Not me. No, ma'am, I'm a cab driver. I don't work just for you."

"Well, I don't need you all the time."

"Still . . . it's expensive to hire me for a whole day. If you had someone just for you, maybe someone who could also do other things for you, it might be cheaper."

"Oh, I'm just fine."

She can't be reasoned with. I give in to the Stockholm syndrome beginning to take hold. "So where do you want to go today?"

She pulls out her list and refers to it. "The mechanic's first."

"Mechanic? You don't have a car."

She laughs then, and I have to admit that her joy is contagious. "No, I just need to talk to the owner. He's a nice young man, and he's not married."

"Not more men."

Callie's smile fades. "I just don't want her to be alone for Christmas."

I know she's talking about Sydney. "Well, can't she spend it with you?"

"Yes, but I'm not that exciting." She offers a faint smile. "I want her to have a good Christmas. She's been sad since her father died. I wasn't that big a fan of his, you know. He never liked me. After my daughter died, he never brought Sydney to see me.

It wasn't until she grew up that I had any relationship with her at all."

"How old was she when she lost her mother?"

"Eight."

"And her mother was your daughter?"

"Yes."

My heart jolts. What a sad thing. In a softer voice, I ask, "What happened to her?"

Her face transitions slowly into sorrow, as if she's living through it again, and her eyes mist over. I wish I'd never brought it up.

"Cancer."

"I'm sorry. That's awful."

"Sydney was such a precious child. I was close to her until then. After that, hardly anything." Her sorrow gives way to a joyful smile. "But God is good. I prayed for her every day, and look what he did with her! And eventually he got us back together."

"Yes, ma'am." As I drive, I think of Sydney as an eight-year-old child, losing her mother and being kept from a doting grandmother. Even if her father was the greatest man on earth, which he couldn't have been if he ejected Callie from his life and Sydney's, the loss of those two women would leave a huge void in Sydney's life.

I go through the motions again as she hits up the owner of the mechanic's shop. She strikes out again.

Her upbeat mood is waning as I get her into the car again.

"Miss Callie, I know you're trying to help Sydney, but why don't you just enjoy Christmas Day with her and stop all this matchmaking?"

"I need to get her a grand present."

"I think you did that yesterday. We went to Macy's, remember?"

"No, I want to get her something she really wants. Not just some old grandmother gift."

"Well, okay. Where do you want to go?"

"That orange place. Where they sell those computers and whatnot."

"Orange place?" I try to think of someplace with an orange sign. "Best Buy?" I ask, even though it's yellow.

"No, no. They have those pod things."

"The Apple store?"

"Yes, that's it. Take me there."

I chuckle and turn toward the mall.

In the Apple showroom, Callie asks me, "Which one would she like?" Her question makes me feel inadequate. She's looking at the iPads. I don't have the cash for one of these puppies, so I have no idea what they cost. There are at least six variations.

"Honestly, you got me."

"Well, which one would you want?"

"Just get her the one you like. I'm sure she'll like whatever you pick."

Callie laughs way too loud. "I wouldn't know the first thing about these things. I just know they're very popular."

The Apple salesperson approaches, wearing his trademark black T-shirt and holding his digitized cash register in the palm of his hand. "She wants to buy an iPad," I tell him. "Could you show her a few of the models?"

Of course he starts with the most expensive model. "This one comes in two sizes, and you can get a keyboard case and a pen to go with it."

"My granddaughter is a lawyer," Callie says, smiling up at him. "She's very pretty. Are you married?"

"Um . . . yes, ma'am. But if she's a lawyer, she might really like this one, and the bigger version might be really handy for her with the pen."

Callie looks at me. "What do you think?"

I wonder if she remembers my name. "Me? Oh, yeah, I think she would like that a lot. It's kind of pricey, though."

"You can pay for it right here," the guy says. "All I need is a credit card."

I don't want to get involved, so I clear my throat. "I'm going to step outside for a minute, get some air. Let me know when she's ready."

I go outside to an iron bench on the sidewalk and drop onto it. I hope Callie isn't frantically looking through her purse for her credit card. I don't want her to be embarrassed.

He hasn't wheeled her out to me yet, so maybe she's actually making the transaction. She's been much more lucid today. How does that work? She could hardly hold a thought the first day I met her, but now she's purchasing the latest tech gadget.

What could be wrong with her? Is it Alzheimer's that comes and goes, or some other kind of dementia that gives her good days and bad days? Or was she just feeling so awful a couple of days ago that it affected her memory?

The tech guy leans out the door. "Sir? She's ready."

I get to my feet. "Already? Really? That was way too easy."

I step back into the store and see the white Apple bag sitting on her lap. Callie is smiling like a contest winner.

"Did you get what you wanted?"

"Yes. We can go now, sweet boy."

I roll her out to the car, get her into the back seat, and hook her in. She holds tightly to her bag the whole time.

"She'll like this," she says as we drive away. "It's the first time I've bought her anything she'd really like."

"I'm sure everything you've given her is nice."

"No. Sweaters and perfume, mostly. Nothing that makes her face light up."

"Well, I can promise you she'll like this one."

I glance into my rearview mirror. She's smiling as I drive. I find myself smiling, too. "Home now?"

"Not yet," she says. "One more place."

"Where to?"

"I need a tree."

"A tree? What kind of tree?"

"A Christmas tree!"

I groan and shake my head. "I'm afraid I can't do that, Miss Callie. I'm not set up to carry trees. No can do."

An hour later, I'm driving away from the Christmas tree lot with a six-foot tree netted on my roof.

CHAPTER 14

Sydney

The judge, who has an iron bladder, doesn't give us a recess until three thirty, and as I'm hurrying to the ladies' room, John Darco blocks my way.

"What do you think you're doing?" the mogul demands.

"Going to the restroom, sir."

"No, I mean in there. With my son. That lawyer is killing us, and you're just sitting there."

"We'll get our chance."

"But the witnesses are saying horrible things about Steve. They're making him seem like a spoiled rich kid who does whatever he wants."

I find myself speechless. It's as if there's something blocking my throat, cutting off my words. I need the Heimlich maneuver. Somehow I clear my throat and force my voice to work. "We'll shoot that down when I cross-examine them," I say. "Believe me, they'll see him as a Boy Scout when I finish."

"In the meantime, they're taking all these shots, and the jury is sitting there lapping it all up."

"Steve is very good looking." That's the best thing I can think to say about him. "I made sure we have young women on the jury. Trust me, they're going to side with him." Even as I say the words, I realize I'm a traitor to my own gender. I hope college girls aren't that stupid. I hope they see right through him.

But my whole case rests on their being hypnotized by his blue eyes.

How did I get here?

I check my watch. "Mr. Darco, I have to hurry."

He raises his finger and points in my face. "If my son loses this case, I'm never doing business with your firm again. Do you understand that?"

"Yes, sir, I do. It's just that this is a tough case, since he actually did bring the alcohol and ram his car into the BK."

I know right away that I shouldn't have reminded him of that.

"I'm warning you," he says.

"Yes, sir." I feel like I need to bow, but instead I skirt around him and hurry into the bathroom.

When I return to the courtroom, Steve isn't there. I hope he makes it in time. While I'm waiting for him, his father comes back to me. "I was thinking," he says in a whisper. "You need to dig up dirt on those witnesses. They're college students. There must be a ton of stuff you can use against them."

"We've looked for things to discredit them," I say. "There isn't much."

"Then make it up!" he hisses. "They're practically kids. You can say whatever you want and they can't prove differently. Knock them into the dirt if they testify against my son."

I'm a little sick. "I can't lie, Mr. Darco. I don't want to be disbarred."

"Real lawyers know how to do it without doing it," he says through his teeth. "Do your job."

Steve rushes in as his father returns to his seat. His shirttail is out, and his dirty hair has fallen back into his face. He reeks of marijuana.

I gape at him. "What did you do? Get high in the bathroom?"

"No. I just ran out to my car for a minute."

"They'll smell you from the jury box!"

"Hey, you told me to quit drinking. It's legal in Colorado."

"It's not in Missouri. We still have five minutes. Go wash your hands and face." I dig into my bag for the gel I gave him this morning. "Slick some more of this on your hair to cover the smell."

His eyes are red and a little puffy. I'll have to make it look like he's been crying. I'll pretend to comfort him when he gets back. I wait, practically holding my breath. As the jury is reseated, Steve stumbles over a shoelace as he heads back to the table.

My days are numbered. I'll be in the unemployment line by New Year's Day.

CHAPTER 15

Finn

My mood has gone south by the time I get Callie home. She's napping in the back again, so I go up to her door and grab her key from under her mat so I don't have to wait for her to find it in her gigantic purse.

I get the stupid tree off my roof and drag it into the house. Then I wake her and get her out of the car. "Miss Callie, I've already put the tree in your living room."

"What tree?" she asks.

I really don't want to do this. "Never mind." I take

her to the door and get her inside. Unfortunately, she sees the tree still netted on the floor. "Oh, bless you! I have a stand in the attic."

I'm ready for this. "No, ma'am, I'm not going to your attic. I have to go. This was supposed to be my day off. I just came over to get paid, and somehow I wound up—"

"Pay you? Yes, I need to pay you."

I tell her what she owes me for today. As she digs out her checkbook, I say again, "Miss Callie, you're spending way too much on having me drive you around. You should hire an assistant who can help you at home and drive you. I'm way too expensive."

"You're worth it," she says as she slowly fills in the blanks on the check. When she's finished, she tears off the check and hands it to me.

I take it, figuring it will probably bounce, along with the other one I haven't cashed yet.

"My attic door is in the hall."

"No, ma'am. I can't go to your attic."

"But how will I stand it up? How will I decorate it?"

"Ask your granddaughter. I'm sorry, Miss Callie. I have to go now. I'm glad you're feeling better."

"Thank you, sweet boy." She takes my hand and won't let it go.

"I hope Sydney likes her Christmas present."

Her face lights up again. "I want you to come for Christmas. I want you to see her face when she opens it."

"I appreciate that, Miss Callie. But I can't. I have plans for Christmas Day."

"What are they?" she demands to know.

I laugh at her pushiness and think of telling her that I'm not going to be Sydney's Christmas fix-up, that Sydney doesn't even like me, that she probably doesn't have any trouble getting her own dates, and that eating with the two of them sounds like the most depressing way to spend Christmas I can think of.

Truth is, I want to spend it watching a recorded UFC fight I've been saving and pretending it's like any other day.

"I have plans with family," I lie.

"Your mother?" she asks.

"No, ma'am. My mother died a few years back."

"A grandmother? Aunt?"

I didn't expect her to get so specific with her

questioning. I don't like lying about a day that's supposed to be holy. Even though I'm no more than an ambivalent believer in the events that Christmas celebrates, I don't want to invite some kind of Christmas curse.

But how can it get any worse? I've spent Christmas the same way for the last few years—almost as if I've been punishing myself for my treatment of my mother, who loved to make Christmas special every year. I don't deserve anything nice on that day.

Maybe spending it with Callie is just what I deserve. Maybe that *is* the Christmas curse.

"I'm going out of town," I say, thinking I'll do just that to make it true, even if it's to the next town over. "I'm sorry, but again, I appreciate your thinking of me."

She just smiles as if she knows I'm ditching her.

CHAPTER 16

Finn

The next morning my Stockholm syndrome is working full-tilt. Patty Hearst had nothing on me. Callie has made herself a daily fixture in my life. She's like gum on the bottom of my shoe. There's no way to get it off without making a mess.

When LuAnn called me before I even logged in for the day, I lit into her. "LuAnn, if you're calling to tell me that I have to drive Callie again, you might as well know that I'd rather drive my cab off a bridge. It's someone else's turn."

"She asks for you, Finn." LuAnn is enjoying this

way too much. "Except she refers to you as 'that sweet boy.' How can I say no to that?"

"Like this. No! No, no, no. Do you know that she made me get her a Christmas tree yesterday? I had to strap it to the top of the car."

"It's just that she needs to go to the doctor again, and you're the only one of my drivers who won't just drop her off at the curb."

The doctor? Why is she going back to the doctor? Is she sick again?

"After what you told me about last time, I thought maybe you wouldn't mind. But don't worry. I'll call Butch."

I imagine Butch taking care of her. He's a brillo pad of a man who's usually ramped up on caffeine and is always looking for a fight. "No, he can't handle her. How about Lamar?"

"No, he's off today. Finn, she's a sweet old lady. Can't you do it?"

I sigh loud enough for her to hear it. "All right, LuAnn, but this has to stop."

"Keep the meter running. She has been paying you, hasn't she?"

"Yes." It's true. Her checks didn't bounce, and I

was actually able to pay my rent. But I like having time between fares to think and be on my own.

Still, I don't want some grouchy cabbie to drop her at the curb outside the hospital. "Okay, I'll take her."

"Thank you, Finn. I knew you would."

I hang up angry and grab my jacket.

The doctor's office is the same as last time. I roll her in and go through the arduous process of getting her checked in. Instead of parking her there alone, I sit down next to her this time, intent on waiting it out as long as I have to. While she seems somewhat lucid this time, she's a little weaker than before. Her shoulders are more slumped, her hands more limp, and her breathing sounds a little heavier. I reach to the magazine stack sitting on the table next to me and pull out one about parenting. Mindlessly, I open it to an article about potty training. When I realize what I'm doing, I drop it back on the stack. I wipe my hands on my jeans as if the magazine has soiled me.

Yeah, I'm losing it.

I turn to Callie. "So this appointment, is it something that you made because you aren't feeling well, or is it a follow-up to the one you had before?" Either she doesn't want to answer or she doesn't know the answer. She just looks up at me. Her eyes are red, but I don't know if that's age or illness or fatigue or what. I haven't really stared into her eyes that much before.

Callie turns her attention to a woman carrying a baby. "You know, some babies just aren't that cute," she says way too loudly.

I glance at the mother, hoping she didn't hear. She didn't seem to. Stifling a smile, I say, "Miss Callie, that wasn't very nice."

"My Gloria . . . beautiful baby."

"Sydney's mom?"

"When she had her baby, I didn't think she had the sense to take care of her. She made a lot of mistakes. Her biggest one was dying too soon."

A blind person with a seeing-eye dog walks by, and Callie is distracted again. "Imagine bringing a dog into this place," she says.

This time I know her target heard her. I think of getting up and standing against the wall where no one knows I know her, but suddenly the door to the examining rooms open and the nurse calls out, "Mrs. Beecher?"

I jump up, thankful. "That's you." I unlock her wheels and push her toward the door. When I've rolled the chair to the nurse, I stop. "I'll be out here waiting."

"You don't want to come back with her?" she asks.

Haven't we been through this before? "No. I'm just her ride. In fact—" I slap my pockets for the phone number I've written down. "Whatever her family needs to know, you should tell Sydney, her granddaughter. I think she's already been in touch with you."

The nurse looks a little concerned. "When I called this morning, Mrs. Beecher said she would have her granddaughter with her."

The doctor's office called her? No wonder she didn't mention it yesterday.

When the nurse takes her, I go back to the chairs and sit there, jiggling my knee, hoping the appointment doesn't last too long. Today's a big day for Christmas travelers since school is out. I don't want to miss this surge in the taxi market because I'm sitting here in this godforsaken waiting room.

But the wait is long. Two hours pass, and I find

myself watching the soap opera on the TV in the corner of the room with the sound turned down. I wonder if Callie's sitting alone in an exam room or if they're actually doing something. Finally, I catch the nurse when she comes out to call the next patient.

"It's been a long time. Is Callie Beecher still back there?"

"The doctor sent her for an MRI and a PET scan," she says. "She's waiting to talk to the doctor again."

I should have known. They must have a back way to slip people out without their cab drivers knowing.

Now I feel stupid for waiting here. I could have been working. I force myself to wait longer.

Finally, after another twenty minutes, Callie is wheeled back to me. She seems weaker than ever. She's wiping her nose with a wadded tissue.

"It's very important that the doctor talk to a family member," the nurse says. "He tried to call her granddaughter, but he just got voice mail. Is there someone else?"

"I think her granddaughter is in court."

"Then he really needs to talk to you."

"Trust me. I'm not your guy. Aren't there HIPPA laws?"

"If the patient is with you and approves our talking to you, then we can."

I feel cornered. "No, I don't want to know. I'm just some guy. None of this is any of my business."

"Okay, sir. Take it easy."

Looking at me like I'm dangerous, the nurse retreats back through the mystery door.

Callie is quiet as I wheel her out to my car and put her into the back seat. It isn't clear to me whether she's been crying or just has a runny nose, but she seems to stare off into space as I get behind the wheel. I look back at her. "Miss Callie, are you okay?"

She doesn't answer, and I wonder if she's even heard me. I'm pulling away when she finally speaks up. "I need to go to church."

I glance in the rearview mirror. "Miss Callie, it's not Sunday."

I wonder if her need to go to a holy place is based on some kind of bad news that she's gotten at the doctor. I almost wish I'd found out . . . then I snatch that thought from my brain. I can't get involved in this. Whatever it is Callie is going through, I'm not going to be pulled in or entangled.

"I know," she says. "I need to talk to my pastor."

My heart jolts. It is bad news. "Okay," I say. "What's the name of the church?"

I recognize the name and head that way. What is going on with her that she needs to talk to the pastor? Does she need someone to pray for her?

Worry suddenly tightens my chest, but I shove it away. I don't have time for this.

But as I drive, my thoughts drift back to the sad justifications I made when my own mother was dying. What is wrong with me?

By the time I get to her church, I half expect her to be asleep, but she's awake and staring out the window. I help her back into her wheelchair and roll her in.

The secretary greets her, then gets the attention of the pastor, who hurries out of his office to welcome her. He rolls her into the office and sits down with her. "I'll wait for her out in the hall," I say.

The pastor waves at me, so I go to the bench I passed in the hallway and drop down. I'm glad Callie is talking to someone if she's upset. Someone better than me. I hope he offers her some comfort, maybe prays with her.

I feel uncomfortable in this house of prayer, as if the people in that office are going to recognize me as an intruder. If they knew me, I'm sure I wouldn't be welcome here.

After a few minutes, I hear her voice and the pastor laughing as he rolls her out. "Miss Callie, I would love to come to your house for lunch. But Christmas Day is just impossible."

Are you kidding me? She's here trying to set him up with Sydney?

If Sydney only knew what this crazy woman is doing!

"You only have to be there for an hour, Pastor," she says. "Just one hour."

"My mother would never forgive me," he says. "But seriously, I'm so glad you asked. I appreciate it very much. I'm sure Sydney's very beautiful."

"You don't know what you're missing," she says with that coy smile.

I'm ticked off as I take Callie back. She looks disappointed as I roll her into the hallway.

When we're on our way home, I look into the

back seat. "Miss Callie, Sydney doesn't need you to do all this. She has a lot going for her. Why are you so dead-set on fixing her up? Don't you think she has men asking her out all the time?"

"I just don't want her to be alone for Christmas."

"She won't be. She'll be with you, won't she? I'm sure that's all she wants."

Callie grows quiet again. Finally, she says, "But what about next year?"

I don't know what to say. Callie doesn't expect to be here next year. Maybe she did get bad news at the doctor's after all. I wonder how long she has to live.

A sudden sadness falls over me, and I can't shake it away. It's that same sadness I felt that day standing at my mother's hospital door. The sadness that drove me back to my car and away from that place.

But I can't get away from Miss Callie.

She's sound asleep by the time I get her home, so I leave the car running, get the key out from under the mat, and unlock her door. Then I go back and lift her out, grabbing her purse to hook over my wrist. She weighs less than a child.

I carry her inside, walk through the house, and

lay her on her bed. Carefully, I slip off her shoes and cover her up with a blanket I find on the bench at the foot of her bed.

I back to the doorway and stand there with tears in my eyes . . . tears that aren't for her so much as they are for my mom.

I wipe them on the arm of my jacket and go back out to the car. I get her wheelchair, bring it in, and set it up next to her bed.

I don't like my unsettled feeling as I lock the door and return the key to its hiding place.

CHAPTER 17

Sydney

I'm having the answering service for Dr. Patrick search for him since he's already left for the day, and I have to know why he's been trying to call. I was in court until five, then had to go back to my office to prepare for tomorrow, and now I'm stepping out of the practically abandoned building into the night. In the parking garage, I'm almost to my car when a limousine pulls up next to me.

A backseat window rolls down, and Mr. Darco peers out at me. "Get in," he says.

I can't believe this. "Mr. Darco, I'm waiting for

an important phone call, and I still have a lot of work to do before court tomorrow."

"Get in, I said. Now."

I want to remind him that we're not the mafia or government spies, we're just embroiled in a stupid lawsuit. But instead of talking back, I get in like an obedient puppy.

The limo is almost the size of a bus, and I wonder why Mr. Darco feels he needs this. Does it help him wheel and deal?

"Mr. Darco, what can I help you with?"

"I got you some dirt." He slides a file across the seat.

"On what?"

"On the witnesses against Steve. One of them cheated on a final exam. Another one abused his girlfriend."

"So . . . there's documented evidence?"

"No, not documented. But they don't have time to dispute it."

"So these allegations are not true?"

"Consider them true."

I almost laugh, but I restrain myself. "Mr. Darco, you've been a part of enough lawsuits to know about discovery. I can't just introduce new evidence that hasn't been shared with the other lawyers. And honestly, even if we discredit these witnesses, there are fifty more. Everyone at the party that night was a witness."

He bares his teeth like a bulldog, his lips wrinkling. I expect him to growl. "Lady, if you lose this case and make my son look bad, so help me, I will ruin you."

"I'm well aware of that," I say. "Mr. Darco, I'm a good attorney. If I weren't, they wouldn't have put me on this case. You need to trust me. I have some evidence that will discredit these witnesses, or at least plant some doubt in the minds of the jurors, but I won't lie."

He slams his fist against the leather wall, and I jump. "Where are the lawyers who know how to win?"

I want to tell him that they're all working on his corporate cases, avoiding this one with all their might.

"If you don't take care of this, I will take care of it myself."

I frown at him. "What do you mean by that, exactly?"

"Never mind. But their stories are going to change before you get them back on the stands. I'll take care of it. Get out."

I'm sick as I get out of the car and watch the limo drive away. He's going to do something illegal, and I don't know how to stop it.

My head is cracking to migraine level as I drive out of the garage.

CHAPTER 18

Finn

Tonight sleep is like a treasure that's just out of reach. The light from the alarm clock seems magnified in my room, and the green light from my DVR shines like a beacon. I throw washcloths over both of them to block out the light and try again. But sleep won't come.

What if Callie isn't okay? What if the doctor's office hasn't called Sydney, and Callie is stuck in bed, sick, with no one to take care of her? What if the news was bad? What if she's terminal?

I get up at three a.m. and make eggs Benedict, something I only do when I can't quiet my brain.

The act of cooking calms me, but I can't get Callie out of my mind. What is wrong with me? I'm the prince of a guy who ignored his mother when she was dying and pushed away the guilt.

But you're thinking about it now.

Where do these thoughts come from? Maybe they've been lodged in some corner of my brain for years. Maybe the guilt has metastasized until it's popping up like a tumor, and I can't push it away.

Maybe Callie is my chance to set things right.

I eat the eggs Benedict without even noticing the taste, and tell myself I'm losing it. Callie is driving me insane. She's just an old lady who has wedged her way into my life, not some cosmic do-over that will absolve my sins.

Still, I can't get her out of my mind.

Hours later, when I've logged in with LuAnn, I decide to go by Callie's house and see if she's okay. The front door is still closed, and I knock loudly enough for her to hear. I wait, but there's no sound inside. I test the knob, but it's locked.

I start to return to my cab, but then turn back. I bend and look for the key under the mat. There it is, right where I left it.

I unlock the door and step inside. "Miss Callie?" I call. "Hello? It's Finn, the cab driver. I just wanted to check on you."

When there's no answer, I step into the kitchen and see that there's a plate in the sink and a pot of coffee that's still warm. *That's enough*, my gut tells me. *She's fine. Go now!* But I can't make myself leave. "Miss Callie!"

No answer, so I move cautiously up the hall and peer into her bedroom. Her bed is made, and there's no sign of her.

Where could she be?

Could Sydney have taken her somewhere? Doubtful. I go back outside, lock the door, and return the key to its place. As I walk to my car, I see her neighbor in the yard, on his knees in the dirt. "Excuse me," I say.

The man looks up. "Yes?"

"I'm looking for Miss Callie. She doesn't seem to be at home. Have you seen her this morning?"

The old man struggles to his feet, dusts himself off. "Yeah, I saw her wheeling off down the street on her scooter this morning."

"Down the street?" I ask. "Really? How long ago?"

"Couple of hours," the man says.

"Does she do that often? Wheel off like that?"

"Never saw her do it before, but you know Callie. She gets her mind set on something, and there's no stopping her."

I get back in my cab and drive slowly up the street, looking for her. There's no sign of her. I go around the block, then drive up and down the surrounding streets. She's nowhere.

Okay, this isn't my problem. I need to stop this right now. But she's clearly sick, and maybe out of her mind. She could be hurt or in trouble. Her phone battery could have died—or her scooter battery—or she could be lost.

When I finally give up looking for her, I find Sydney's number. Of course it goes to voice mail. I wait for the beep. "Voice mail, who would've expected that?" I say. "This is Finn, your grandmother's personal driver. Your grandmother seems to have disappeared. She was seen wheeling off down the street on her scooter a couple of hours ago, and I can't find her anywhere. She obviously shouldn't be out by herself when she can't walk and she's sick and probably doesn't know her own name, but hey, maybe you disagree. If you have any idea where she might have been trying to go, how about giving me a call? But if the whole job thing is just too much of a priority, we'll wait until someone notifies you of what became of her, since you are her only family."

I'm talking way too loud as I finish the voice mail, and I catch my image in the mirror and realize my face is red. I click off the phone and try to calm myself. I picture Callie out on the street, confused, trying to find her way home.

Maybe I should call the police.

I drive around some more, not wanting to take another fare that might tie me up. Finally, my phone rings. I don't recognize the number.

"Hello?"

"Finn? This is Sydney, Callie's granddaughter. We just recessed for lunch and I got your message. Have you found her yet?"

"No, I haven't."

"I'm on my way over," she says. "Where could she be? She's not in her right mind. I saw her this morning, and she was confused and weak. I don't know how she would have even gotten that thing out the door without help!"

"According to her neighbor, she was alone."

"Are you sure *he's* in his right mind?"

"I don't even know the guy!" I yell.

"Well, what are we going to do?"

"We? Lady, I'm not responsible for her. I was just checking on her because she seemed so weak last night, and it was clear she got bad news at the doctor."

"Please. Meet me at her house. I might need to call the police. I need you there because I don't know where you've looked."

I let out a hard, loud sigh and turn my car around. "All right. I'll be there in a few."

Sydney's car is in the driveway when I get there, and she's sitting on the porch steps. She's dressed in a severe navy-blue jacket and matching skirt that looks binding and restrictive on her.

Why do professional women so often think they have to dress like men?

I get out of the car and walk across the yard. "How ya doing?"

"I'm worried," she says. "I talked to her neighbor, and he told me what he told you. At least he's sticking to his story. I guess he wouldn't do that if he had short-term memory loss or something."

"You have a nice way of giving people the benefit of the doubt."

"Hey," she says, getting to her feet. "I didn't want it to be true, that she wheeled off down the street on her scooter that hasn't been charged in days. I wanted to think that maybe she got another cab and went somewhere."

"She didn't. I checked with dispatch."

"Maybe she got an Uber."

"Seriously? You think she could navigate an app on her phone?"

"Maybe. If her mind is lucid."

"Sorry. Not buying that. She would have called me."

Her voice is getting weaker. "Well, maybe not, if she wasn't lucid."

"Make up your mind. Was she making sense at breakfast?"

"I couldn't tell. She was quiet. I got her up and dressed and fed her. Then I put her in her chair and turned the TV on. She wasn't herself."

"So you left her there? Nice going."

"I had court today! I'm trying—"

"She needs full-time care. You know that, don't you?"

"She hasn't been this bad until recently, and there's not much money. I've been trying to do it myself, but I'm obviously doing a horrible job."

"Always some very good reason," I say. "Take it from me. You can always justify not being with someone who depresses you because they're not how you like to see them. But one day they're just gone, and then there's nothing you can do about it."

She clearly doesn't appreciate that. "I don't need to be lectured."

"I'm not lecturing you. Just sharing some experience."

She bursts into tears now, something I didn't expect from someone who has tried so hard to look tough. I don't know what to do. Do women want to be held when they cry, or do they want you to pretend you don't notice? Do they even want you to look at them?

I don't know, so I go with my gut. I sit down next to her. "She's probably just visiting a friend."

She wipes her tears. "She's outlived all her friends, except for the ones at church. She's homebound, so she doesn't see them that much, and I don't think any of them live near here."

"Maybe she forgot someone died and went to see them anyway. Want to go look?"

She nods. "Yeah. Let's go."

She clicks to my car in her heels and gets into my passenger seat.

"So where should we go?" I ask, getting behind the wheel.

"What do you mean?"

"Which friends? Where did they live?"

Tears well again, and she shakes her head. "I don't even know."

I pull a tissue out of my console and hand it to her. "No one? You didn't know a single one?"

"Stop judging me!" She dries her eyes and pulls herself together. Taking a deep breath, she says, "I remember some man who lived down the street. He had all this yard art. Trolls and stuff around a fountain."

"Her boyfriend?"

"No. He was the widower of a good friend of hers. But he died a couple of years ago. I guess she could have gone there to visit either one of them. Someone else lives there now."

I pull away from the house and head slowly down the street, looking for the yard art.

"There!" she says about ten houses down. "That's the fountain. They got rid of the trolls. I'll go to the door."

She gets out, and I watch her knock on the door. She talks to a young woman who answers with ankle biters clinging to her legs and a tiny dog yapping at Sydney.

She doesn't look happy as she comes back.

"No luck?"

"No. They haven't seen her."

I sigh. "Okay, where else?"

"I don't know. Wait, there's a house on the main road. Turn left up here."

I follow her directions. "The house up here on the corner. She's mentioned that she used to have a good friend who lived there. I don't even know her name."

I pull to the curb in front of the house, and Sydney gets out again. She goes to the door, but no one answers. She's about to come back to the car when a woman comes around from the backyard. I roll down the window and hear Sydney asking if an old woman on a scooter has been here. The woman says she hasn't seen her.

Sydney is angry and red-faced as she gets back in. "Nothing. You would think that someone would have seen her rolling down the sidewalk on her scooter."

"Any other ideas?"

"No! I don't know who her friends were before I reconnected with her. I don't know where she would have wanted to go!"

"Take it easy," I say. "We'll just drive around and we're bound to spot her. She can't have gotten far."

I go up and down the streets parallel to and adjacent to her house, but there's no sign of her. We stop every time we see someone out and ask if they've seen her. She's vanished into thin air.

The longer we look, the more upset Sydney gets. My idea that she didn't care about her grandmother was wrong. She's about to lose it.

"I don't know what to do. Maybe we should call the police." She checks her watch. "Oh no. I'm going to be late for court. I'll lose my job."

"If someone fires you because you were looking for your missing grandmother, you shouldn't be working there anyway."

She turns to me. "Really? You think so? Do you know what would happen if I lost the first job I've had in a law firm? After all that education, all that hard work, all the student loans that I'll work for the rest of my life to pay back . . . ?"

"So you said there were layoffs, right?"

"Yes. And I'm next. When my current case is over, they'll decide whether to keep me. But if I don't show up to court, it's over."

"Surely you don't think all those who were downsized are going to have to find another line of work. They're attorneys, too. They'll get hired by other law firms. So would you."

"I'm in the middle of the stupidest case in the history of lawsuits," she mutters. "It's a losing battle. I can't possibly win, and just by representing this guy, I'm risking my reputation. But I have no choice. This guy got drunk at a dorm party—which he provided the alcohol for—and then he crashed into a Burger King. He's suing the college and the Burger King. Two separate cases."

"No way."

"Yes."

"And you agreed to take that case?"

"I wasn't given a choice. He's the son of one of our biggest clients. If I win, I'll be a hero."

"But it can't be won."

"Not if the jury's sober. And when this case is over, if I don't get laid off, I'll have to do the second case—against Burger King."

"That's insane. Why would a judge even allow this case?"

"I was hoping he wouldn't. See what a terrible lawyer I am? I was hoping my case would be dropped. But this case is the only reason I wasn't laid off with the others. Sometimes I feel like I'm in the middle of a mudslide."

"How's that?"

"I feel like I'm hanging on to a stump for dear life as the mud just slimes down around me. Uprooted trees are drifting down in all that mud, hitting me in the head and knocking me black and blue, and I'm still hanging on, covered with mud and slime . . ."

"This is some analogy."

"And any minute the ground below my stump is going to turn to mud and my stump will go under, and I'll go down with it into a pile of mud."

"Probably wouldn't be a pile. More like a swamp or lake. Maybe a pond."

"It's my metaphor. Do you even hear anything I'm saying? Do you understand it?"

"Of course I do. I used to be in the restaurant business."

"How does that have anything to do with this?"

"I understand the desperation of feeling like everything is crumbling. Or sliding . . . as it were."

I turn onto another residential street about three blocks from Callie's house. Still no sign of her. "That's the reason I'm driving a cab now. All that stress and craziness. It was killing me. Owning a restaurant—"

"You owned a restaurant?" She looks shocked.

"Yeah. I was St. Louis's Chef of the Year for three years in a row. Success went to my head. I decided I had to have my own restaurant, so I opened one, hired a new chef, and suddenly I'm working eighteen-hour days and juggling bills and staff and customers, instead of cooking. Did all right for several years, but then the economy tanked, and people preferred burgers to haute cuisine."

She pulls her chin back and frowns at me. "You cook haute cuisine?"

"Did. If I'd been cooking all the time, I might

have been happier. But I was doing things I hated. Got to the point that I wanted to run away. Somebody offered to buy it, and the price was enough to pay my debts. And I never want to go back into that business. After all the training, all the experience, all the passion. I put my life and relationships on hold, and in the end, the business failed me."

"But . . . you could have just gone back to being a chef. Worked for someone else."

"Burnout is a real thing. You should take my advice. Get out while you still like your profession. Don't let yourself be stuck with something you hate."

"I can't quit, and I don't want to be fired. I have goals. There's a lot at stake. You don't understand." She gets her phone out of her purse and tries Callie's phone again. "Still voice mail!"

I hear a *thud*—a sound no driver wants to hear—from my right front tire. "What now?" I get out of the car. Leaving my door open, I go around to that tire and stoop down. It's flat. There's a brick a few feet behind it.

Sydney gets out of the car.

"A brick," I say. "Who leaves a brick out in the

street like this?" I stand up and look around for the culprit. Maybe he's hiding in the bushes, laughing his head off. Probably some sadistic kid.

"We don't have time for this," she says.

"Ya think?" I fling back. I go to my trunk and yank up the rug over the spare. "Just shoot me. The spare is flat." I slam my hand against the fender. "I'm gonna have to call a tire service."

"We can't wait for that! Finn, I have to find her! I need to call the police."

"Just hold on," I say. "Let me call dispatch, see how long it'll take for them to get someone to help me."

She gets back into the car and texts frantically, tapping her foot on the floorboard as I call LuAnn. "I'm sitting here on Cooper Road, and my tire is flat," I tell her. "And guess what? The spare is flat, too. Who was responsible for getting it fixed?"

"I don't know," she says. "I'll have to look back through my records."

"No, don't bother, LuAnn. I don't have time. Callie is missing. I have to find her."

"Callie, the old woman? Where did you lose her?"

I exhale heavily and look at Sydney. "I didn't lose her. She's just lost."

"I can get a service to you in about an hour."

I groan. "LuAnn, her life could be at stake. Please, can you send me a cab to take us back home so we can get another car?"

Sydney's poking at her phone. What's she doing? Checking Facebook?

"I'll send you a cab," LuAnn says. "But the closest one I have is about twenty minutes away."

"What? Twenty minutes? No! You don't have anybody in this part of town?"

"I had you there," she says.

"Well, I would pick myself up, except I have a freakin' flat tire!" I yell.

"Finn, you don't have to get huffy."

Sydney holds up her phone for me to see a map with a little dot moving. "Don't worry about it," she whispers. "I got an Uber. He'll be here in three minutes."

She might as well have slapped me. I gape at her.

"I'm not waiting twenty minutes," she says. "You don't have to come with me, but I'm taking an Uber back to my car."

I'm livid now. "This, LuAnn, is why people use an app to get a ride. Send someone to change my tire. He'll have to bring a spare. I'm not going to be here. I have to go help find her."

"Will do, Finn," she says. "I'll forgive you for your tone because you're the only one I have who works the geriatric crowd."

"There it is now," Sydney says, pointing as the car pulls up.

I set my chin and click off the phone, and stare at the tiny ten-year-old Civic that idles in front of us.

"His name is Jeff," she says.

Something about that makes me even madder. I lock my car and stroll toward the Civic. I open the front door as she gets into the back. "Hello, Jeff."

"How ya doing?" he asks.

"Not great."

"This is really funny," he says as I buckle myself in the passenger seat, in case this kid runs off the road. "An Uber driver picking up a cab driver." He leans into me and lifts his phone for a selfie. "Can I take a picture to post on Instagram?"

I push his hand away. "No, Jeff, you cannot. Now, do you want to know where we're going?"

"No, I already know. It's in the app." He snaps

a pic of my debilitated cab anyway, still chuckling. "This is classic."

Sydney isn't bothered by this at all, and why would she be? She clearly doesn't know the difference between a cab and an Uber. Try getting Callie into the back seat of one of these.

She calls the police as we're driving, reports Callie missing, and asks them to meet us at her house.

"They should be there shortly," she says when she hangs up. "I have to send someone to court to tell the judge I have an emergency. Who's at the courthouse?" She apparently comes up with someone and gets them on the phone.

I check out Jeff's phone as he follows its GPS to Callie's street, and I watch the little dot of our Civic crawling through the map. I hate this guy and everything he stands for as we turn into her driveway.

I reach for my wallet.

"Don't," Sydney says. "I already paid him on the app."

"I can at least tip him," I mutter.

"I did that, too."

I frown back at her. Seriously? She can do all

that on her phone? I look at Jeff, who's smiling with oblivious naiveté. How many people are actually going to tip if they don't have to look a driver in the face as they hand it to him? How many will even remember to do it?

"We're way more convenient than cabs," he says, chuckling. "No offense. You should get the app."

"No thanks." I get out and open the door for Sydney. She's enjoying this. I'm glad my discomfort has given her a distraction from her mudslide.

"Don't even," I say as we go to her car.

"I won't," she says. "But oh, I want to."

Thankfully, a police car pulls up as Jeff backs out of the driveway. Sydney tells them her grandmother has vanished. The cop goes back to his car and radios something in. As we wait, she takes off her jacket. She looks more relaxed, even though I know she isn't.

"You should lose those jackets for good," I say. "You look better without them."

"It's not a beauty contest," she shoots back. "I have to look professional."

"You're not going to look like a man no matter how hard you try. You can be a professional woman without following the male dress code."

"So I'm supposed to take fashion advice from a guy in a backward baseball cap?"

I grin.

The cop gets out of his car and walks back up the driveway. "I found her."

"What?" Sydney says. "Where?"

"At Missouri Baptist Medical Center. She collapsed on Torrence Drive and someone called the hospital."

"Torrence?" I ask. "How did she get that far?"

"Is she all right?" Sydney asks.

"She was taken by ambulance. I can put you in touch with the EMTs who transported her."

Sydney is about to collapse herself as I usher her into her car. As we head to the hospital, she calls one of the EMTs and puts it on speakerphone. "Hi," she says when he answers. "I was told you transported my grandmother to the hospital this morning? Callie Beecher?"

"Yes, I transported her a couple of hours ago," he says.

"Is she all right? Is she alive?"

"She was stable when we got her there."

"What happened?"

"It looked like her battery died on the scooter, and she was trying to walk away from it. The lady who saw her fall said she was very unsteady. She saw her faint."

"She's too weak to be walking," Sydney cries. "She's been really sick."

"She was still on the ground when we got there," the EMT says. "I don't think she'd hit her head, but she was in and out of consciousness."

Sydney is quiet as she gets off the phone and stares through the window as she drives to the hospital. I take a stab at making her feel better. "The other day, when she was locked out, I took her to eat lunch at Lulu's. We sat down and she said, 'Thank you, Jesus.' I thought she was confused about who I was."

She smiles a little. "She loves Jesus. She talks to him a lot, right out loud. She did that even before she had this . . . confusion."

"Are you sure it wasn't one of the first signs of it?"

"Yeah. It was just her way of praying. Jesus was . . . is . . . very real to her."

I get quiet, not wanting to make a joke of that. I'm not sure why.

We're silent as we get to the hospital, and she

pulls into a space near the front door. I get out when Sydney does.

"You don't have to come," she says. "I know you have to get back to work."

"I want to make sure she's all right," I say. "I'm coming in."

I follow her to the information desk in the emergency room, and she gets Callie's exam room number. "Only two family members can go back at a time," the nurse says.

"It's just the two of us," Sydney says without telling her I'm the cab driver.

We walk up the hall to Callie's room. Sydney opens the door, and we step inside. Callie is in a hospital bed, looking very small. Her eyes are closed, and she doesn't stir at the sound of the door.

"Grammy?" Sydney says, shaking her.

Callie doesn't wake.

"Maybe she's on medication," I say.

Sydney goes back to the door. "I want to talk to the doctor."

I stand at the door as Sydney goes up the hall to the nurses' desk. "Who is Callie Beecher's doctor? I need to see him."

"He's on the floor," I hear the nurse say. "I'll tell him you're here."

Sydney comes back to the exam room. "She looks like she's dying," she whispers.

Her phone rings before I can answer, and she pulls it out of her purse. "Oh no. It's my boss." She swipes it on. "Mr. Southerby, I'm so sorry I had to ask for a continuance, but I've had a family emergency. My grandmother vanished, and then I found out she was taken by ambulance to Missouri Baptist. I'm here now, waiting to talk to the—"

The boss cuts her off, yelling so loudly I can hear it from across the room. It's almost enough to wake Callie, but she still doesn't stir.

"I know, sir," Sydney sputters. "No, I do want this job. I know they wanted it over by Christmas, but I'm the only one my grandmother has . . . I will, sir . . . No, I have every intention—"

The doctor steps into the room, and Sydney swings toward him. "I'm sorry, Mr. Southerby, but I have to go." She hangs up on him, though he's still talking. I want to cheer.

"What's wrong with her?" she asks the man in scrubs.

He's carrying a laptop, which he sets on the table and opens. "I'm glad to finally meet you. We've been playing telephone tag."

"Did she hurt herself when she fell?"

"No," he says. "Yesterday we had her come back in because our test results were worrisome. We did an MRI and PET scan. Today we did X-rays, and there are no fractures. We understand she fell onto grass, so there don't seem to be any injuries from the fall. We think her condition precipitated her fainting."

"What condition?" Sydney asks. "A UTI would cause unconsciousness?"

"Her condition, and her collapse, are caused by late-stage cancer," he says.

I catch my breath. Sydney reaches for the footboard of Callie's bed to steady herself. "Late stage . . . ?"

"Yes."

"Wait." She shakes her head, as if trying to clear it. "Are you sure you don't have her mixed up with someone else?"

"Callie Beecher. Trust me, this is not a woman you easily forget. You didn't know?"

I stand rigid, staring at him, feeling as if I don't belong here. But I can't make myself walk out.

"No! Why didn't anyone tell me?" Sydney asks.

"I tried to call multiple times," the doctor says.

"I tried to call you back last night. I was in court all day."

"I can't leave a message like this on voice mail," he says. "Your grandmother has liver cancer that has metastasized all over her body. She has masses in her lungs, her pancreas, her stomach, and her brain."

Sydney starts to cry again, and I step toward her but don't touch her.

"No!" she says. "I thought the antibiotics were helping her. I thought—"

"She does have secondary pneumonia. We started IV antibiotics today. But as I said, she is in late-stage cancer."

Sydney clutches her forehead. "So . . . we'll do chemo, right? Radiation? We'll fight this."

The doctor glances at me, as if to tell me to help Sydney with this, but I just stand there, like I do.

"She's beyond chemo. While she was still clear-headed, she opted to forgo it. It wouldn't have offered her much more time."

I take off my cap and ask, "How long does she have left?"

"We don't like to put a time on these things."

"Ballpark," I insist.

"A year?" Sydney asks. When she sees the sympathy on the doctor's face, she says, "Months? Weeks?"

"At this point, after this episode," he says softly, "I think weeks would be optimistic."

"Days?" The word cracks in her throat, and she seems to lose her legs and begins to fall. I grab her then and help her to steady herself.

She rallies her strength and looks at her grandmother. "Days," she whispers. "She has days left, and I couldn't even take the time to take her to the doctor or answer his call."

She pulls away and bends over the bed, touches her grandmother's face, strokes the wrinkled skin. "Grammy," she whispers, and tears assault her again.

I look awkwardly at the doctor. "Is she . . . is she going to recover . . . from this episode? Or is this it?"

"She may recover some strength and be able to go home. The next few hours will tell us. We'll do our best to get her home for Christmas if we can.

I know it's important to her. She's told me more than once."

I wonder if she tried to fix him up with Sydney.

"We're going to set her up on hospice care, but since it's so close to Christmas, we may not be able to get it started until the day after Christmas."

"Hospice?" Sydney says as though that word rips her to shreds.

"We want to keep her comfortable."

I can't stand here anymore. I tell Sydney I'll be in the waiting room, but she doesn't seem to hear me. I go out there, get a Coke out of the machine, and look around for the least germy seat. There's a kid sitting close to the vending machines who's covered head to toe in a rash, so I head the other way and sit by the woman with a swollen ankle.

I try to get interested in a Dr. Phil episode on the TV in the upper corner of the room. It isn't turned up, so I try to follow the conversation on the closed captioning, but it's several seconds behind the voices. Soon I'm just staring at the screen, not reading lips or transcription. Just thinking about Callie lying on the ground, then being loaded into an ambulance.

I should have talked to the doctor yesterday. I should have tried to reach Sydney. I go into the men's room and bend over the sink. I turn the water on, splash it onto my face.

When I go back to the waiting room, Dr. Phil is off and a soap opera is on. I don't know why I'm sitting here. I should be working the airport crowd. What is wrong with me?

The doors to the ER open. Sydney stands barefoot, looking around the waiting room. She looks spent, and her blouse's shirttail is outside her skirt now. She's carrying a bag.

I stand up. "Sydney?"

She turns and looks relieved as she comes toward me. "Hey. I figured you were still here."

"Is she okay?"

"Yeah, she woke up. She even knew me. They're moving her to another floor. They told me it would be a half hour or so."

"Want a drink? Something to eat?"

"Yeah. I missed lunch."

I realize I did, too. "We could go eat high hospital cuisine. Or something out of the vending machine."

"The cafeteria, I guess."

We head to the cafeteria, neither of us speaking as we get our food. We both wind up making salads at the salad bar, and we reach for the same salad dressing. "You first," I say.

She puts some on hers, then finds a table. When I'm finished prepping mine, I take the seat beside her. We both eat quietly for a moment.

When she looks at me, she says, "I wanted to thank you."

"For what?"

"For doing what I should have done."

"What's that?"

"Taking her to the doctor. I should have—"

I touch her hand, stopping her. "Don't."

"But she kept calling you, and you kept coming. You didn't have to. You could have refused. And you were kind to her. You cared."

I'm getting uncomfortable now. She's starting to think more of me than I deserve. "Look, you don't have the market cornered on this. I've had my share of regrets about what I didn't do for someone in my life . . ." My voice trails off, and I don't have the stomach to finish.

"She has cancer," Sydney says. "How could I not know that? How could I not be there for her?"

"I think you have been."

"Not when she needed me most. I'm sorry. You're a nice guy, but really? The cab driver is the one who's taking better care of my grandmother than I am?"

"Come on. I drove her around. I even charged her for it. Don't give me too much credit on the whole caretaking thing."

Her eyes glisten as she locks her gaze on mine. "It was more than that and you know it." She takes another bite, then says, "My mother died when I was young. I adored Grammy. She was my biggest fan. But when Mom died, Grammy tried to get custody of me. My father won the court battle, but he was so angry that he decided to never let her see me again. He could be vindictive and unfor-giving sometimes, which is probably why Grammy thought he wouldn't be a good single parent. But I had memories of her."

"So when did she come back into your life?"

"A few years ago. When I was getting close to graduating from college and had gotten into law school, I thought that my mother would have been so proud. And then I wondered if Grammy was still living, and I went looking for her."

"She must have been thrilled."

"She was. She had prayed for me all those years. She had never given up on seeing me again. But I haven't held up my end. I've tried, but I wasn't used to someone focusing on me the way she did. Until she got sick, I didn't spend that much time with her. Then she started needing help . . ."

"And apparently you were there then."

"I go by every morning and every night, trying to make sure she's okay and taken care of."

"Sydney, that's a lot. That's so much more than . . . a lot of people do."

"Not enough. She had cancer, and I didn't even know."

I can't dry her tears, but I decide to do my best to make her smile again. "I'll never forget that morning I took her to the doctor the first time. A nurse walked by, and Callie asked someone if her own thighs were that big."

Sydney almost chokes on her food as she laughs. "Sounds like her."

"Another time she commented, very loudly, on the likelihood that a woman passing by was going to lose her marriage, since her husband was better looking than she was."

"She does talk loud, doesn't she?" She's giggling now. "She hasn't had much of a filter for a while."

"Did you know she's been making me drive her around to see men?"

"*Men?*"

"It's true. At first I thought she was hitting on them, but she was visiting them for you. She's invited each of them to spend Christmas with the two of you. She even invited me."

Her smile fades like air going out of a balloon. "Do you think that's because she knows she won't be here next Christmas?"

"I'm sure of it."

She sighs. "She thinks I can't make it on my own."

"I'm sure she just doesn't want you to be alone." I grab her tray and stack it on mine. "I'll take this, then I'll get out of here. If you feel like it, text me to let me know how she's doing."

"Okay, I will." I start walking away, and she says, "Finn."

I stop and turn back.

"If she gets out in time for Christmas, you should come."

I swallow hard and nod. "I'll think about it."

"Okay. Thanks for helping me look for her."

"No problem."

I watch her walk from the room. She's still barefoot, and she looks nothing like a lawyer, except for the skirt. I hope she doesn't pick up some kind of foot fungus.

As I wait for LuAnn to have someone bring my cab, I look up toward the upper windows and whisper a prayer that Callie will make it home for Christmas.

CHAPTER 19

Finn

I stop by Walmart to buy some food and notice a floor model of a small tabletop Christmas tree that's marked half off. It's already decorated with white lights and some red, shiny balls. I buy it and carry it out, and lay it carefully on my back seat. I hope it will put a smile on Callie's face if she's awake when I go back.

Back at the hospital, I trek up the hall with it to Callie's room, knock lightly, and push the door open. She's sound asleep on the bed, an oxygen tube clipped under her nose. I look around for a place to put the tree, but the bedside table is cluttered, and there's a plastic pitcher and a Styrofoam glass of water on the rolling tray table. Across the room is a cheap, hospital-grade chifforobe. I set the tree next to it on the floor, then realize she won't even be able to see it unless she sits up.

I go out to the hall to look for a box or something to put it on. As I pass the nurses' station, I lean over and get a nurse's attention. "Could you tell me if Callie Beecher is alone, or is her granddaughter still here?"

"She's still here," the nurse says. "I think she's in the prayer room. She asked me where it was. It's down the hall to the left. There's a cross beside the door."

"The prayer room?" I say. "Okay." I don't really want to go to the prayer room, but I do want to know how Callie is. And since I'm not family, no one but Sydney can tell me. "Listen, do you have a big box lying around somewhere back there?"

"A box?" she asks.

"Yeah. For a little Christmas tree. Just to get it high enough that Miss Callie can see it."

"No, I'm sorry. There isn't anything."

"Don't all those sheets come in boxes? Or the

drugs? Or those cheap little off-brand tissue boxes that cost twenty times what they cost in stores?"

"Excuse me?"

I don't know whether she can't understand me or if she's being deliberately obtuse. I give up on her and head down to the prayer room. I'll peek in, and if Sydney isn't in the throes of prayer, I'll ask her about Callie's condition. But when I crack the door open, I see Sydney sitting on the second row, leaning forward with her head bowed. She may be crying.

I step back into the hall and slip into a tiny waiting room where I can watch the prayer room door. I pick up a *People* magazine and flip through without reading until Sydney comes out, wiping her eyes.

It's probably not the best time to approach her, so I wait, wondering whether she got more bad news about Callie. My heart sinks. What should I do? I'm suddenly drawn to that room. It won't kill me to go in and pray. I cross the hall and step back into the quiet. There's no one else here.

Something about the warm silence in the room draws me inside. I slip into the last pew and look at the front, where a life-sized nativity scene is displayed.

My mom used to take me to church before I got too smart to believe in Jesus. I quit going long before I should have. Actually, I liked sitting next to her and smelling her faint perfume and the smell of Spray Net in her hair. And I still have questions that were never answered. Like why would the creator of a vast universe make his newborn son sleep in a sheep's feeding trough? Animals around him—did he even notice them? Or did Joseph spend all night shooing them away from the manger?

And what is a stable anyway? Probably like a horse's stall, just a few feet wide, and Mary had to sleep in smelly hay.

When I raised questions like that as a seven-year-old kid, my mom got impatient and told me I was being disrespectful. But I really wanted to know. Eventually I stopped caring, but now I find that awestruck curiosity returning.

The young parents who barely knew each other, the tiny, naked newborn whose first look at the earth was the same one the goats had when they were born. And then there was the whole cross thing, which baffles me when I give it enough thought.

As I think about that scene today, I feel a little homesick.

A man slips in and sits a couple of rows in front of me. I stay there until he finishes his brief business with God and slips quietly out, leaving me alone and reminding me that I have business here, too.

I lean forward, elbows on my knees, and rest my face in my palms. "If you could just answer one prayer," I whisper. "It's not about me. Well, maybe it is a little." I clear my throat. "If you could just help Miss Callie. She's a funny old lady, and she deserves a nice Christmas." I rub my eyes, surprised at the moisture there. "Guess you know even better than I do what a person deserves. Didn't mean to suggest you didn't. Just . . . feeling a little awkward."

I stay in that hunched posture, lingering under the authority of quiet. Thoughts of my mother ambush me again. I look up at that scene at the front, the scene of a family who probably had no grasp of what they were getting into. I wonder if the baby had some deep knowledge even in that manger, or if he just had the normal thoughts of a newborn . . . cold, hunger, touch . . .

It doesn't really matter what he knew then.

What matters is what he knows now. I'm suddenly hit with the absurdity that I would be asking him for anything, a person like me.

"I know I've done things wrong," I whisper. "If you could just help me not to get it wrong this time."

I don't know if he hears or cares, but somehow it feels like he does. "Thank you, sir," I whisper after a few minutes pass.

I slip back out of the prayer room and dab at my nose. I must be allergic to something in there. Dust or hay or some chemical pew cleaner . . .

I take a deep breath, pull myself together, and drive to the closest store—a Home Depot around the corner from the hospital. I don't find a table small enough to work in a crowded hospital room, so I grab two plastic bins with tops. I can stack them on top of each other. I go down the Christmas aisle until I find a festive tablecloth. I can toss this over the bins. Then when Callie goes home, she can use the bins for whatever stuff she's collected during her stay—fifty-dollar Kleenex and hundred-dollar plastic bedpans, and the pitcher that ought to be made of gold for what she'll be charged for it . . .

I hurry back to the hospital and find Sydney

sitting beside Callie's bed. I step inside. "Has she been awake?"

"Briefly," she says. "Come in."

I bring the bins in and stack them up next to where I left the tree. "I won't be long. Just wanted to get this set up."

"It was you who brought the tree?"

"Yeah, only there wasn't any place to put it. I didn't want to use her tray table."

She watches as I stack the bins and cover them with the tablecloth. Then I put the small tree on it. It won't reach a plug, so I move it a couple of feet and plug it in. The lights come on, reflecting off of the red balls.

Sydney smiles. "That's beautiful. Thank you, Finn. She'll love it."

Callie opens her eyes now and looks around at us as if her mind is waking up.

"Grammy?" Sydney says. "Hi."

Callie takes her hand. "Sweet girl," she says.

I walk to her bed, hands in my pockets since I don't know quite what to do with them. She turns and looks at me. She smiles and reaches for my hand. I give it to her, and she pats it, too. "Sweet boy."

"Finn brought you a Christmas tree," Sydney says.

Callie tries to sit up, her wizened face all smiles. "Oh, it's beautiful! Look at that." She looks around. "Is this the hospital?"

"Yes," Sydney says. "Do you remember the ambulance coming?"

Callie lies back down. "I was fine. They could have just taken me home."

"Miss Callie, why did you go out alone?" I ask.

She lifts her chin. "I wanted to go for a walk."

I chuckle. "On your scooter?"

She doesn't seem to see the humor in that. "Well, I'm fine now." She tries to sit up, but Sydney makes her lie back down. "It's not Christmas yet, is it?"

"No, Christmas Eve is tomorrow," Sydney says.

"They're going to let me go home, aren't they? I'm fine. I have to be home for Christmas. I have big plans."

"Grammy, I'm not sure if you're going to be strong enough to go home. But don't worry, we can celebrate here."

"No," she says, sitting up again. "I have to go home. I need to talk to my doctor. What's his name?"

"Dr. Patrick," Sydney says. "But, Grammy, you have pneumonia, and you need the IV antibiotics. It's really important."

Callie seems not to hear her. She turns to me now and squeezes my hand. "You have to come for Christmas. I won't take no for an answer."

I give her a smile, then meet Sydney's eyes. She doesn't want me to promise her she'll be home, I can tell. "Miss Callie, if the doctor lets you go home for Christmas, I'll be there. But if you're still in the hospital, I'll come here."

"Wonderful!" she says, clapping her hands. She looks back at Sydney. "We're going to have such a time, aren't we, sweetie?"

Sydney doesn't know what to say. "Grammy, we'll have fun no matter what."

"I have a big turkey and my famous sweet potato casserole and the best dressing you ever tasted . . ."

I wonder how in the world she has cooked those things in the condition she's been in.

"And I got you a present that you're really going to like. Not like those things I've bought you other years."

"Grammy, you didn't have to get me anything.

Seriously, it doesn't matter about gifts or food . . . as long as you're feeling better."

"Oh, I feel better," Callie says. "I haven't felt this good in years."

In spite of my better judgment, I let myself believe that's true.

CHAPTER 20

Finn

The phone wakes me the next morning at seven a.m., and I fumble around for it and swipe it on. "Hello?"

"Yes, is this Finn?"

"Yeah, who's this?"

"I'm a nurse at Missouri Baptist, and Mrs. Callie Beecher asked me to call you."

I sit up in bed. "Miss Callie knew my number?"

"I had to call your taxi service and get it. But she was pretty insistent. She wanted me to ask you if you could drive her home when she's discharged this morning."

"Discharged? Is that a good idea? She's been pretty sick."

"The doctor wrote discharge orders after seeing her a few minutes ago. It'll take a couple hours to get the paperwork ready and fill her prescriptions, but then she'll be ready to go."

I slide out of bed. "Yeah, I'll give her a ride. But where's her granddaughter, Sydney? I thought she was spending the night there. Did you talk to her?"

"She's already left for work. I'm sure Mrs. Beecher will be in touch with her. She probably would have called you herself if she'd had your number."

"Don't assume anything about Miss Callie, okay? Sydney will need to know this."

"I'll take care of it," the nurse says. "So you'll be here when she's discharged?"

"Yeah. Tell her I'll come."

When she hangs up, I look at the phone for a minute and drop back down onto the bed. So Callie conned the doctor into letting her go. Sydney isn't going to like it.

I find her number on my contacts list and call her. It rings to voice mail, as usual.

After the beep, I say, "Yeah, Sydney? This is

Finn Parish . . . cab driver? The nurse just called to ask me to drive your grandmother home when she gets discharged this morning. You know about that, right? I just . . . wanted to make sure." I sit there a minute, trying to think of what else to say, but I finally hang up.

I head to the hospital, and as I'm getting onto the elevator, my phone rings. It's Sydney. "Hey," I say.

"You cannot take her home!" Her voice sounds like she's walking fast, and she's breathing heavily. "And what is a nurse doing calling you? I'm the next of kin. If they're going to let her go home, I need to know, don't you think?"

"That's why I called you. I guess Callie made them ask me for a ride."

The elevator opens, and I step off and hear Sydney's voice coming out of the elevator next to me. "What she needs is IV antibiotics and a hospital bed!"

I put my phone down and talk directly to her. "Hey, I'm just the messenger."

She jumps as she sees that I'm right in front of her. She drops her phone into her bag. "They think she's in her right mind, but she's not! And that doctor. Why does he have such a hard time calling family members? What is it with this guy?"

I follow Sydney down the hall, letting her continue her meltdown. When we get to Callie's room, the door is open and we can see the nurse standing over Callie's bed, making her sign some forms.

"Stop!" Sydney says as we go in. "She is not going home today. I want to talk to the doctor!"

"Sweet girl . . . ," Callie says with a sly grin.

The nurse looks confused. "The doctor discharged her."

"Call him now. I'm her next of kin and I have her power of attorney."

"Okay. I can have you sign her forms."

"Can't you see she's sick? She has pneumonia and she's confused and she has cancer. There must be pain and discomfort, and she needs oxygen and—"

"I'll call him," the nurse says and scurries out.

Callie reaches for me. I walk to her and take her hand.

"Are you taking me home?" she asks.

"Miss Callie, Sydney doesn't want you to go."

"Don't be silly," she says. "I have a million things to do. They said it's Christmas Eve. I'm not spending it here. Tomorrow's Christmas!"

Sydney has tears in her eyes now. She's breaking my heart. "Grammy, you're so sick. I know you think you have to do some grand thing for Christmas, but we can do it here. I promise, I'll make it special. I'll spend the whole day with you."

"I'm not making you celebrate Christmas in the hospital. I'm going home."

Callie looks at me, and I stay quiet. It doesn't seem like a good idea to get between them.

The nurse's voice comes over the intercom. "Ma'am, I have the doctor on the phone. Can you come speak to him?"

"Yes, I'll be right there." Sydney turns to me. "Don't take her anywhere. I'll be right back."

I smile at Miss Callie as she leaves. If the old woman could walk, I have no doubt she would be racing out of here. Thankfully she just stays on the bed.

CHAPTER 21

Sydney

My grandmother is too sick to go home!" I tell the doctor in a voice that's too loud. "The fact that it's Christmas should have no bearing on your medical decisions for her."

The doctor sounds as if he's put me on speakerphone and is standing across the room from the phone. I can barely hear him. "Ma'am, we're starting her on oral antibiotics today, and we're prescribing pain medication that will get her through the holiday until I can get a hospice nurse to visit her. I gave her the choice, and she was pretty insistent that she go home for Christmas."

I'm shaking now. "But I should have been the one to make the choice. She's not in her right mind! She's here because she wandered off on her scooter and collapsed. She can't make sound decisions."

"She seemed clear this morning."

I want to throw the phone. "Are you blind? She's got dementia!"

"As I said, she seemed—"

"Please take me off speakerphone," I bite out. "I can't hear you, and this is an important conversation!"

I know I'm getting too excited, and my temper is throbbing in my chest. If he were here, I might physically hurt him. But I have to lower my voice before they throw me out.

Dr. Patrick takes his phone off speaker and speaks directly into it, like a normal human being who wants to be heard. "Is that better?"

"Yes," I say. "Thank you."

"Sydney, the thing is that keeping your grand-mother here isn't going to make much difference. She's relatively stable right now. There's no reason she should miss her last Christmas. She only has a short time left, and she doesn't want to spend it in the hospital. This Christmas holiday has some special significance to her. I can't in good conscience keep her here when it's so important to her, and it makes so little difference."

My heart sinks. "But maybe if you kept her on oxygen and IV meds, you could prolong her life. Maybe she could actually get better."

"She's not going to get better. I'm sorry, but I thought I was clear about that."

The fight drains out of me, and I feel myself physically wilting. My face twists into that ugly cry face, and my throat is so tight I can't speak.

"Let her have Christmas at home," he says. "Keep her comfortable. Give her what she wants. Enjoy every minute with her."

I suck in a sob. "You're just giving up!"

"I'm not giving up. I'm going to do whatever I can for her. But that includes giving her the best quality of life I can for as long as she has left."

I finally give up on the doctor and hang up the phone. The nurse appears in the hallway. "She all set to go?" she asks with too much cheer in her voice.

I storm past her without answering as I go back to Grammy's room.

CHAPTER 22

Finn

I'm waiting in Callie's doorway when Sydney comes back up the hall. As she approaches, I see the pink blotches under her eyes, as if she's taxed her tear glands to the max. The tip of her nose is also pink, and she's clutching a Kleenex in her hand. I hate seeing her like this. It does something to me.

I start to ask if she's okay, but the moment our eyes meet she throws up her chin and says, "Okay, let's get this ball on the road."

I grin. "You mean, 'Let's get this show on the road'? Or 'Let's get this ball rolling'?"

She looks at me with disgust instead of amusement. "Are you finished?"

"Sounds like you are. What did the doctor say?"

"She's going home." She goes into the room and unplugs the Christmas tree, moves it to the center of the floor, and starts to pack up Callie's few things that Sydney brought from home.

"Okay, Grammy," she says. "Looks like you win. You're going home for Christmas." She looks like she's about to chew someone's head off, so I tread softly behind her.

"Am I driving her home?" I ask carefully.

"If you don't mind," she says. "I need to make sure one of my colleagues can go to court to ask for a recess. Then I'll be there to take care of her." She's throwing things into the bag now. She goes into the bathroom and grabs the toothpaste and toothbrush. "And you really are coming to Christmas lunch tomorrow, right?"

"Are you okay with that?"

She turns her livid eyes to me. I wonder what happened on that telephone call. She's certainly looking for a fight. "You're coming. That's final.

She's going to be home and she wants a significant Christmas and she would like for you to be there."

I clear my throat. "I told her I would come, so I guess I will."

"Pardon me?" Callie says in a weak voice.

"I'm talking to Finn, Grammy." Sydney turns back to me. "No guessing," she says. "My grandmother wants you there. She insists on being home for Christmas, and by golly, she's going to have the kind of Christmas she's been fantasizing about. Any questions?"

"Okay, you're obviously upset. What did that doctor say to you?"

"Oh, nothing," she says. "He basically just told me that I have no say in the matter, power of attorney or not. And that it doesn't make much difference whether she's here or there . . ." Her voice breaks off now, and tears push back into her eyes.

I reach out and touch her shoulder. She freezes for a minute, then resumes packing things up. "Do you think you can get everything in the cab?" she says more softly. "Even the tree?"

"We could leave the tree here," I say. "Maybe

some other patient would like it. She has one at home. It's still netted, just lying on the floor, but . . ."

Sydney shrugs as if she couldn't care less. "Really, I'll only be gone for a little while. I just have to move for a recess until after the holidays, even though I'm sure the partners are already plotting my demise."

"Take your time," I say. "I'll hang out with her till you get there."

She dabs at her eyes again as if it would be a mortal sin to be caught with tears rolling down her face. "Look at you. The cab driver, of all things. You're acting like a family member. More of one than I am."

"You're doing fine, Sydney."

"No, I'm not," she says. "I haven't even been around enough for the doctor to feel like he needs to tell me the most basic things."

I want to touch her again, but I resist the instinct and let her zip up the bag.

The nurse comes back. "Well, it looks like we're all set."

"Thank you, precious," Callie says to her as if the nurse has always been the most helpful one in the building.

"I've got a cart out in the hall," the nurse says. "Hold on just a sec."

Callie is beaming, but her face is pale and she has dark circles under her eyes, and her breath comes in short bursts. I worry that she's not getting enough oxygen.

The nurse comes back in with the cart, and we start loading the things onto it.

We've almost got everything ready when Sydney's phone chimes. She looks annoyed as she checks it. "Oh no. My boss. I have to take this."

I help Callie into her coat as Sydney walks out into the hall. I can hear her from in here. "Yes, sir . . . No, he didn't call me. Why? . . . He did? On Christmas Eve? In broad daylight?"

I grin, imagining what she's talking about. A Christmas party where someone got out of control?

"It's just that my grandmother is being released from the hospital at this very moment, and she's not in good shape . . . Yes, I want my job, but maybe someone else could go take care of it . . . Of course I'm on the team . . . No, I understand. I'll . . . I'll be right there . . . No, sir. I can be there within the hour."

She looks up at me, and I see the distress in her eyes.

"But tomorrow is Christmas. I'm supposed to be with my grandmother. It may be the last one."

Tears take over again, and she squints her eyes shut and pinches the bridge of her nose. "No, sir . . . Yes, I'm sure that can be worked out . . . Of course. Thank you, sir."

I step out into the hall as she clicks the phone off. "Did that end well?" I ask.

She swings around, not even bothering to hide the tears now. "No, it didn't."

"You have to work tomorrow?"

"Yes. No. Maybe, I don't know. I'm just . . . not sure. Maybe he's just testing my commitment."

"Testing your commitment? What kind of cruel game is that?"

"It's not a game. He's the most serious man I've ever met." She sighs. "My client, the idiot who's suing the college and Burger King, just got arrested."

"Not good."

"No, it isn't. His father is breathing fire. But it seems to be my problem. Damage control, not to mention getting the judge to set bond so I can get him out in time for Christmas."

"And tomorrow?"

"I don't know. Depends on whether I can even corral a judge on Christmas Eve. I have no choice."

"You do have a choice, Sydney. Someone else could handle this. You need to quit that job."

She forces a sad laugh. "Quit? You're out of your mind."

"I'm just saying that if you're anything like I think, you can do better than this. You worked your way through school. You passed the bar. You landed this job. You can land others. One where they give you serious cases instead of soul-killers, and one where they respect the things that matter to you, like your very last Christmas with your grandmother."

"Don't judge me!" she bites out. "You don't understand!" Her face twists, and she covers it. "Can you just take her and stay with her until I can get there? I'll hurry."

I look down at the floor, not wanting to embarrass her. "Sure."

The nurse pushes past me into Callie's room. I follow her in, and Sydney comes in behind me.

"You can take the cart to the car," she tells me. Then she turns to Callie. "I'll be at your house as soon as I can," she says gently. She puts Callie's bag on the cart, then picks up her own messenger bag and throws the strap over her shoulder. She dabs her eyes again. "Okay, well, I guess I'll go now so I can get back sooner." She looks up at me. "Just be careful. Call me if there's any problem."

Tears are rimming her eyes again as she bends over and kisses her grandmother on the cheek. "Bye, Grammy. See you in a little bit."

"You take your time, sweet girl," Callie says, amazingly cogent.

As Sydney bursts into tears again and rushes from the room, I roll the cart out behind her. The nurse pushes Callie behind us. I try to figure out what's going through Sydney's mind. Is it the imminent death of her grandmother? Is it the loss of control? Is it worry for Callie's safety?

When I move my car to the door, we get Callie into the back seat and load everything into my trunk.

Callie looks happy and wide-eyed as I get into the car. "Before we go home," she says, "I need you to take me by Kroger. I have to pick up my fixin's."

"Your what?"

"The food I'm cooking tomorrow. It's Christmas, you know."

"Miss Callie, you know you don't have the energy to cook, don't you? You can't even stand in the kitchen."

"Don't worry about that," Callie says. "They cooked it for me like they do every year. All I have to do is pick it up."

I frown. "So you ordered an entire Christmas dinner from the grocery store?"

"Yes. Feeds six."

"Six? Who all is coming?"

"Sydney, you . . . You're coming, aren't you?"

"Sure, Miss Callie. I'll be there if you really want me."

"Yes. That pretty lady in the Kroger deli is a great cook, and she said she always cooks mine personally."

I get to Kroger and pull up to the curb in front of the door. "So it's in your name?"

"That's right. Can you get my chair?"

I don't want to take her in. I want to get this over with. "Just stay here, Miss Callie. You need to rest. I'll run in and get it."

"Well, all right."

"Is it already paid for?"

"I think so."

Great. If it's not, I guess I'll have to pay. I get a buggy as I go in and head back to the deli. Others are in line to get their holiday meals, so as I wait I look around for other things Callie might need. I grab some rolls from an endcap and pull a pecan pie out of the freezer.

Finally, I get up to the front. I give them Callie's name, and they bring out a huge cooked turkey in a box, several trays of food, a pumpkin pie, and some cranberry casserole.

Some of the food is still warm. I wheel it away after making sure it's paid for already, then I stop and look under some of the wrappers and take a whiff.

Not bad, but needs a little more. I hurry through the aisles of the store and get a few more spices and the ingredients I could use to make it taste a little less store-bought. I wonder if she has tea bags for iced tea. I buy some. I can get the rest of what I'll need from home.

When I've paid for the extra things, I take the food out to the car. Callie is sound asleep. I put the box of food on the seat next to her. Even the smell and the closing of the door don't wake her.

As I get back behind the wheel, my heart sinks and overwhelming sadness blankets me.

This might be Callie's last ride in my cab.

CHAPTER 23

Finn

I wake up before dawn on Christmas morning and realize I don't dread the day as I usually do. There's a difference between waking up to *Forensic Files* reruns on Christmas morning and waking up with someplace to go.

But as I'm sipping on my coffee, I realize I don't have any gifts to take to Callie's. What do you get someone who's in her final days of life? Besides, who is even open on Christmas morning?

I check on my phone and see that the local grocery store is open 24/7, even on Christmas. Maybe there's something I can pick up there.

After I shower and shave and put on a button-down shirt instead of my usual T-shirt, I almost don't recognize myself. I can't wear a backward baseball cap on Christmas. My mother would turn over in her grave. But that means I have to work a little harder on my hair. I hate that, but I do it.

When I'm presentable, I go by the grocery store. The floral section is at the front, though I've never noticed it before. I scope the place and find two poinsettias. Perfect. One for each of them, and it's not an awkward gift that has to be opened and reciprocated.

I put the plants into my basket and go up and down the aisles, picking up a few more things I can use to improve our Christmas meal. When I'm done, I realize that I don't know what time I'm supposed to go over there. Callie never told me a time. She only said we were eating lunch. It's ten a.m., so I figure I might as well go on.

When I get there, Callie's front door is open. I look through the screen door and don't see her, so I knock and call out, "Miss Callie?"

I hear her calling something back, so I step inside, carrying my plastic grocery bag and the two plants.

Her tree is still lying on the floor in the small formal living room area. I set the poinsettias down and poke my head in the kitchen.

Callie is sitting in her wheelchair in front of the sink. The turkey is in the pan, but I can see that she's having trouble with it.

"Miss Callie?"

"Hello, sweet boy," she says. "You're just in time. I don't know what I was thinking. I'm weaker than I thought I was." She laughs as if she's not bothered at all. "It's cooked but needs to be warmed. I didn't know how I was going to get it in the oven."

"I got it, Miss Callie. You mind if I spice it up a little?"

"You know how?"

"Sydney didn't tell you that I used to be a chef?"

"I . . . don't know. Did she?"

"I picked up a few things from the grocery store. I thought maybe I could take it up a notch."

"Well, aren't you talented?"

I laugh. "Why don't you reserve judgment until you taste it?"

She watches, relaxed, as I work on the turkey, making a basting sauce and reworking the stuffing.

"I had hoped to spruce the place up some," she says, "but for the life of me I can't find my decorations."

"They're in the attic," I remind her.

"They are? How do you know?"

"You told me. And some jerk refused to get them down or put up your tree. But as soon as I get this food in the oven, I'll go up and get them."

She claps her hands. "Oh, you are precious!"

"Yeah, that's what they always call me." I laugh to myself. "Hey, where's Sydney?"

She looks around, confused. "I'm not sure."

"But it's Christmas. She's not still working, is she?"

"Yes. Yes, that's where she is."

"Are you sure?"

Callie looks a little disturbed. "She said she'd be here."

Irritation sweeps over me, but it's quickly chased away by sympathy for Sydney. Something bad must have happened.

I decide I'll just do my best to distract Callie until she arrives.

I set the oven to warm up the turkey, then I pull the steps down from the ceiling and climb the rickety ladder up into the dark, dusty attic. There's a light up there, but the bulb is out. I take my phone out and use its flashlight to see my way, hoping I don't step through the ceiling.

I see a big box that says "Christmas" not too far from the opening, and I grab it and take it down. Then I go back up and find a wreath and a plastic bin containing lights. Another box has the Christmas tree stand, ornaments, and tinsel. I get them all down.

Callie has a grand time looking through the box and pulling things out as I get the tree set up. I wheel her to the tree, and she helps hang the ornaments at seat-level as I string the lights onto the branches. I see a bunch of ornaments with little girls' pictures, and she handles them delicately.

"Those girls. Who are they?"

She gets a confused look in her eyes. "I don't know," she says. "But aren't they pretty?"

I help her hook a vintage one onto the tree. "This looks kind of old. Could this be a picture of your daughter? Sydney's mom?"

Her face lights up. "Yes, it probably is."

"What was her name?"

She looks into the air blankly. She doesn't remember. I quickly change the subject. "This one has to be Sydney. What was she? Three? Four?"

"Yes, must be," she says, smiling again.

I plug in the lights, and she laughs aloud and claps her hands as the tree lights up. Her joy seems so intense that I want to prolong it. "We need some Christmas music, don't we?"

"That would be lovely. Do you think you can find a radio station playing it?"

"I guarantee it. But we can do better than that."

I find a station on a radio app on my phone, one that plays older Christmas songs around the clock. Today is the one day it doesn't bother me. The sound isn't that good without speakers, but I have a hunch that Callie doesn't care. She claps her skinny, vein-clustered hands with the music.

I go back into the kitchen and work on the casseroles. I should have planned to cook myself. I could have made my confit de canard. Duck is always better than turkey, especially store-cooked turkey. And they both would have loved my tarte tatin for dessert instead of Sara Lee's frozen pecan pie.

But I do the best I can with what I have to work

with. I just wish I knew when Sydney will be here. There's nothing ruder than expecting someone to cook Christmas dinner for you and not telling them when you'll come. I fight back my indignation, and then it hits me. I wasn't feeling upbeat about Christmas with Callie. I was really just looking forward to being with Sydney.

Funny how things like that sneak up on you.

It's just a little while later when Sydney rushes in like a brisk wind, carrying a shopping bag with a couple of gifts in it. I'm in the kitchen stirring my cinnamon mixture into the pumpkin pie filling and trying not to crack the crust.

"You're cooking!" she says.

I glance back at her. "You go shopping?"

"No. I had these already."

"So you were working?"

"Yeah, I guess you could say that."

I take the turkey out to make room for the other food that needs to be warmed, and cover it with tin foil to keep it warm until the casseroles heat up.

"When did you get here?" she asks.

"Couple hours ago."

"You decorated the tree for her?"

"Yeah, it was no big deal."

"Thank you, Finn."

I give her a tight smile. "No problem. Did you get Trust Fund Kid out of jail?"

She doesn't answer right away. As she takes off her coat, she says, "I knew it was unlikely that a judge would release him, because he's already built himself quite a reputation for having unparalleled gall."

"Not to mention a penchant for driving drunk."

"Right. Oh, and he coldcocked the arresting officer, gave him a black eye. That didn't go over well."

I'm not mad anymore. I spoon out some pumpkin pie filling and give her a bite. She takes it, then has the exact reaction I hoped for.

"Oh, that's so good. What is that?"

"Old family recipe."

"Really?"

"No."

She laughs and takes another scoop. "It's fantastic. I didn't really expect you to cook."

"Well, I can't eat store-bought food without at least trying to fix it up. It's not so bad now. So the kid . . . did you get him out?"

"I got a judge there, and he set bond at fifty thousand dollars."

"No hill for a climber like his dad."

"Right, except that he was hungover from the night before, and he demanded to know what they'd done with his car, which was now in the impound lot, and he threatened to sue the city . . ."

"For letting him drive drunk?"

"No, for putting a dent in his car, even though he was the one who put it there when he ran into the electric pole, knocking out electricity to an entire neighborhood."

"You're kidding. On Christmas Eve?"

She steals another taste of my pie filling. "And when the judge told him that he was responsible for that damage, he took a swing at him, too."

"Over the bench?"

"No. The judge was standing in the hall. It's informal, this whole thing, but I'm guessing the judge might rethink that in the future. Gave the judge a bloody lip, after which he revoked bond and said he was a danger to himself and others, and ordered him to spend Christmas in lockdown, on suicide watch until after the holidays."

"Uh-oh."

"Yeah." Her smile fades, and she grabs a paper towel and wipes her mouth. "So then the dad comes to the jail to chew me out and everyone else involved, and my bosses, two of the partners, come up there and rake me over the coals. But as hard as I tried, I couldn't do anything about it. He wasn't getting out today."

"He *shouldn't* be out today."

"They don't see it that way. They accused me of ruining a simple thing like bond for a DUI—"

"Like you were the one who swung at the judge?"

"Yeah, and the dad made a big show of leaving our firm, and the partners in turn . . . fired me."

I suck in a breath. "What?"

She's still smiling. "They said I had an attitude problem, that I'd been uncooperative lately, that I was costing the firm too much money."

"They cost themselves all that money by making you take that stupid case in the first place."

"Right? Even Gloria Allred wouldn't take a case with a client like that."

I stare at her more seriously. The red rims of her eyes make sense to me now. I feel bad for thinking the worst of her. All I can think to say is, "Well, at least you got the rest of Christmas off."

"Yeah. And New Year. All of next year too, as a matter of fact."

I try to think of something pithy to say, but nothing comes. "I'm so sorry," I say finally.

She swallows and shakes her head. "No, it's fine. You were right. I should have left there a long time ago. You told me I could do better. You were right. It's just that none of those who got let go have found jobs yet. So . . ."

"You will."

She gazes into my eyes for a moment. "Let's not think about it today, okay? Let's just think about Grammy. She's in there singing and clapping. You made her happy when I was at the jail beating my head against the cinderblocks. You're a nice guy."

"Don't tell anybody." I turn back to the oven and check the turkey.

We go into the living room where Callie is still admiring her tree and clapping to the Christmas songs. When the food is ready, Sydney and I bring it in to the dining room table, and if I say so myself, it's all pretty good. I wouldn't have minded serving any of this at Christmas in my restaurant.

And then it gets awkward. "Thank you, Jesus," Callie says, and this time I know she's not talking to me. "You have always been there for me," she says as she claps her hands again. "And look at us. Sydney here, and this sweet boy."

I suspect that she still doesn't know my name, so I smile and wink at Sydney.

"We had some lonely Christmases. Oh, my church friends were always sweet to invite me, but it wasn't the same as family. But I always knew you'd get me back with my girl. You're good to me. And you'll be good to both of them, too." She giggles a little, then adds, "I like them together."

I close my eyes to keep from meeting Sydney's.

Callie doesn't end the prayer with *amen*. She just claps her hands again and says, "Isn't this fun?"

There's a lot of laughter during the meal, and I remember that first day I had to drive Callie. Never in a million years would I have expected to be here today, enjoying every second.

When we finish dessert, Sydney asks Callie if

she wants to open her gifts. Callie is like a child as we move her from the dining table to the tree, and I know she's excited because she wants to give Sydney her gift. She insists that we start with that, and I find the gift for Sydney on a table. Callie sits up straight in her wheelchair and grins at me. "That other gift, young man, is for you."

I look down at the other box, crudely wrapped by Callie's own hand. There's a tag on it that says "Finn." I look up at her, surprised.

"Go on, open it!" she says.

I wait as Sydney opens hers, and she looks shocked as she unwraps the top-of-the-line iPad. "Grammy!" she says. "How did you know to do this?"

Callie laughs with pure joy and shakes her finger at her. "I finally got you something you like?"

"Grammy, I've always liked what you got me. This is fantastic, though. Really fantastic."

They both look at me, and I take my cue and tear into the wrapping. When I get to the box, I see what it is. Another iPad, just like Sydney's. I just gape at it. "Miss Callie, no. You got me one when I went outside?"

"I wanted you to have one, too."

I feel tears misting my eyes, and I rub my mouth. I don't cry. I won't do it in front of them. "Nobody's ever . . . This is great, Miss Callie. Thank you."

She laughs again and leans back in her chair, as if she's accomplished everything she set out to do. "You're a good, good boy. Your mama would be so proud of you."

Now I lose it. I lean, elbows on my knees, and look at the floor as I fight whatever this is that's twisting at my face.

When I gather myself, I remember that I brought gifts, too.

I give Callie her poinsettia. Sydney seems surprised when I give her one, too. She gives Callie a new robe and bedroom slippers and some little wheelchair accessories to make her life easier.

When we're done, Sydney and I both take our iPads out of their boxes. Sydney's is rose gold and mine is black. I don't even know how to turn it on.

"Here, let me see it and I'll show you," Sydney says.

I wait as she clicks around on my iPad. After a moment, she hands it back. "Here's my Christmas gift to you," she says.

"What is it?" I ask.

She points to an app she's just added.

"Uber."

Her laughter has become a calming influence on me, I have to admit.

"In case you ever get stranded again. I'll put it on your phone, too."

"Gee, thanks," I say.

"And if you want to drive for them, you can do that through the app, too."

"Great."

Sydney laughs out loud. Callie closes her eyes, still smiling.

"Grammy, do you want to lie down?"

"Maybe for a few minutes," the old woman says. "I just need to close my eyes for a bit."

Sydney takes her to the bedroom, and as she gets her down, I clear the table. Sydney comes back and helps me do the dishes.

"So you're the one who helped her buy the iPads?"

"No, I just took her there. The Apple guy sold them to her."

"I don't know why she thinks I haven't liked the

other gifts she got me." She smiles as she dries a plate and puts it into the cabinet. "One time she gave me a scrapbook of my mother's. I had never seen pictures of my mother as a child. Another time she gave me an old stuffed animal that my mother slept with when she was a little girl. I got all emotional and couldn't say anything, and maybe she thought I just didn't like it. But I still have it. It's a treasure."

"She almost got you towels."

"Really? That would have been fine. Everybody needs towels."

"They were plaid."

"Oh. Yeah, she does have a thing for plaid. She got me plaid sweaters last Christmas. Those were probably the gifts she thinks I didn't like because she never saw me wear them."

"She agonized over those towels. Actually did buy them. I wonder what she did with them. Maybe she forgot."

"Well, I love the iPad."

"So do I, but I feel bad about it. She shouldn't be spending that kind of money on someone she hardly knows."

Sydney grins. "But you're her sweet boy."

"I'm the cab driver. Does she realize that?"

"You're way more than that." She puts the last dish on the shelf and makes another pot of coffee. "I hated you the first day I met you. I'm sure you hated me, too."

"I wouldn't say that."

"Yes, you would. You made me feel so guilty. But I don't blame you. You had gone way beyond the call of duty."

"Was Callie like a big powerhouse CEO or something when she was young? Because she can get anybody to do anything she wants."

"She should have been one."

"I'm serious. All those men she made me take her to see. I can't believe she didn't convince some of them to come."

"I'm so embarrassed."

"Don't be. I don't think any of them blamed you."

"But they must think I'm some homely spinster who can't get a man on my own. If I had time for a man, I could have one."

"Oh, I told her that myself."

She looks up at me. "You did?"

"Of course. After I met you, I knew you didn't need a matchmaker. But she was worried about you. Didn't want you to be alone."

Sydney's cheeks flush to pink. "Oh well. Grammy has always wanted to make a great Christmas for me. This year she really got it right."

"Yeah, iPads make great gifts if you can afford them."

"I wasn't talking about the iPad."

I look down at her, trying to think of something quippy to say, but then I realize this isn't a quippy moment.

Suddenly I want to kiss her, and in spite of myself and the warring responses in my brain, I lean over and just do it.

As our lips touch, she sucks in a breath and pulls back, and just as I think she's going to turn away or slap me, she takes my face in her hands and kisses me again.

Those warring voices in my head instantly go silent, and all I can think about is the feel of her lips and the taste and the smell of her . . . I touch her hair, something I haven't even realized I wanted to do.

The kiss is long and lazy and sweet . . . just right. You don't always know it's going to be. I've kissed people before and known instantly I didn't want to do it again. But Sydney pulls me in, igniting a craving that scares me a little.

And all I can think as I hold her is that Callie Beecher rocks.

CHAPTER 24

Finn

After we put the food away, we sit beside each other on the couch and play with our iPads. Sydney helps me set up my email and download apps I will really use. We're both blown away when we discover we don't need a Wi-Fi connection to get online with them. Callie sprang for the souped-up cellular versions.

We learn each app together, and then we watch each other's favorite YouTube videos and laugh until we shush each other for fear of waking Callie. Then we shoot selfies of the two of us together. I've never taken a selfie in my life before this.

Finally, we realize hours have passed, and Callie hasn't stirred. I get up to get another glass of iced tea and offer to get Sydney one.

"You don't have to serve me. We're not in your restaurant."

"You look thirsty," I say.

She gets up. "I'd better go check on Grammy."

She heads down the hall as I go into the kitchen. As I'm putting ice in the glasses, I hear her calling urgently, "Grammy!"

I turn and step into the hallway. "Everything okay?" I call.

"Grammy, wake up!" Her voice sounds broken, raspy.

I hurry down the hall to Callie's bedroom and see Sydney bent over her grandmother. Callie looks like she's still sound asleep, but her face is a pale gray, and her lips are colorless.

Sydney's crying. "She's . . . I don't know what . . . Grammy, please . . ."

I put my arms around Sydney and hold her for a minute. She's shaking so hard I don't know how her legs are holding her up. She pulls free and tries again to wake her, but Callie doesn't move.

I touch the old woman's face. Her skin is so cold. I don't want to check for a pulse, but someone has to. I move my fingers to that place on her neck and wait. Nothing. I move my fingertips and wait again.

I turn my helpless gaze back to Sydney, and she covers her face and breathes in a deep, dreadful sob that pulls something from me. I leave Callie and go to Sydney again and pull her against me, letting her weep against my shirt while I bury my face in her hair.

Minutes pass while my brain races for a thought it can't quite grasp. Finally, I realize we have to call someone. I pull out my phone, call 911, and tell them that Callie is unresponsive. I tell them to hurry, even though I can see that it will do no good. I surprise myself when tears come to my eyes as I tell them she has no pulse.

"I should have been here all day," Sydney says. "I should have let Steve fend for himself."

"Shhh," I say, stroking her hair. "She had the day she'd been looking forward to. She had you here . . . on Christmas . . ."

"And you."

"She had both of us. She successfully set you up.

She gave us gifts and saw how much we loved them. She ate to her heart's content. She decorated the tree and laughed and sang . . ."

We hear the siren coming up the street, and I let Sydney go and look out Callie's window. The ambulance pulls to the curb.

Sydney goes to the door to let them in, and I stay with Miss Callie. I lean over and press a kiss on her forehead. "Thank you for including me in this beautiful Christmas, Miss Callie," I whisper.

My tear falls onto her wrinkled cheek, and I wipe it away with my thumb. I straighten up as I hear footsteps coming through the house.

"And thank you, Jesus, for giving me a second chance." Callie doesn't hear me, but I feel like someone does.

CHAPTER 25

Finn

Callie doesn't leave the same way she came home. Sydney and I stand apart from each other, watching, shocked, as the paramedics wheel her little body out on the gurney. Her head is covered by the thing they've zipped her into. It looks like a white sheet over her face.

When the dust settles, will Sydney blame me for bringing Callie home when she wanted her to stay in the hospital? Maybe Sydney was right. Maybe they could have saved her.

As the ambulance drives slowly away, taking Callie to the funeral home, I look at Sydney, not sure what she will tolerate from me now. I wait for her to lead.

"Do you think she knew she was going to die today?" she asks.

"When she lay down for that nap? No, she didn't know."

"If she did, I think she was okay with it. All she wanted was Christmas. And that was for me."

I want to say that it turned out to be for me too, but that might be presumptuous. I don't know where all this leaves Sydney and me. Just because we were starting something this afternoon doesn't mean we'll continue it. Callie put us together, but that doesn't mean Sydney will want to stay that way.

Just as I'm about to talk myself out of this whole thing and convince myself that the relationship birthing between us was just in my head, Sydney walks into my arms again. I instinctively let her in, closing my arms around her as she lays her head against my chest, as if she's found a home.

"I never should have wasted one minute of today on that spoiled brat."

"No, no should-haves. She wanted you to be happy."

"I was happy today."

"So was she. Trust me on that. We should all go on a day like this."

She pulls back and looks around as if she doesn't know what to do next. "I guess I have to plan the funeral. What do I do first? When my dad died, my aunt planned everything. I didn't pay attention to the details."

"Maybe you should wait until tomorrow. I'll go with you if you want."

She lets me go and looks up at me. "Are you sure?"

"Yes, I want to."

"Okay."

"Yeah. If you mean it, I'd like it if you came. But what should I be doing now?"

"Why don't you sleep a little? Get some rest. If you just can't, maybe you could write up something to put in the paper."

"Yeah." She looks around Callie's house. The tree is still on, and there's a garbage bag of torn Christmas paper on the floor next to it. Callie's scooter sits against the wall.

"I don't think I can be here. I'm just gonna go home."

"I can drive you."

"No, I need my car. I'll be okay. Will you?"

"Yeah," I say, forcing a smile. "But if you need anything—even just a friendly voice—you call, okay? Doesn't matter what time it is."

"I will."

I feel like it's my cue to go, so when she gets her purse and the things she needs from the house, she walks me out. I kiss her cheek before she gets into her car. She seems a little distracted, as though the weight of reality is beginning to crush her.

That night I sleep with the iPad on the bed next to me. Before I go to sleep, I pray. This is getting to be a habit. "If you could help Sydney . . . It's going to be a long night for her. Maybe you could just zap her with sleep and help her feel better. Let her think happy thoughts."

I'm as surprised as God must be that I'm praying again. I feel as if he heard me. I'll bet Callie has put a bug in his ear for Sydney.

The next morning I call LuAnn to tell her I won't be driving today. "I need a few days off," I say. "I have a death in the family."

"Your mother?" she asks.

"No, not my mother."

"Grandmother?"

"No. LuAnn, can you give me the time off or not?" I really don't want to talk about it.

"A sister or brother? Aunt or uncle?"

"Why do you care?" I almost shout.

"I'm just worried about you. I want to know how bad a shape you're in."

"I didn't say I'm in bad shape. I just need to help with the arrangements."

"Why won't you tell me who it is?"

"Because it's none of your business."

"I might have wanted to come pay my respects."

"You didn't know her. How could you have respects to pay?"

"I know *you*! I go to funerals, okay? I'm a good person."

I don't want to tell her who it is, and I realize my reluctance is making me seem crazy.

"Oh my gosh," she says finally. "It's that Callie Beecher, isn't it? Did she die?"

I squeeze my eyes shut. "Okay, yes. She died yesterday. Are you happy?"

"No, I'm not happy. She was a sweet woman. All

those trips to the doctor. I knew she wasn't doing well. Why did you say it was family?"

"Because I didn't think you'd give me time off for the death of a customer. I had gotten . . . kind of attached to her."

"You old softie. I knew you would."

I sigh. "And I got to know her granddaughter. She's pretty torn up. I thought I could help her."

"Her granddaughter, huh? The one who wasn't anywhere to be found when her grandmother was sent by a cab to the hospital?"

"She had good reasons."

"So you like her, huh?"

I'm getting madder by the minute. "Time off or I quit, LuAnn. Your choice."

"You're so touchy, Finn. Of course you can have time off."

I slam the phone down.

CHAPTER 26

Finn

Because I'm worried about Sydney, I make her muffins before I go to her house the next morning and take her a Starbucks coffee. She's dressed when she answers the door, but I can see that she's already been grieving this morning. "Thought you might be hungry," I say.

Smiling weakly, she steps back from the door and invites me in. "I hadn't even thought about food."

She takes the plate of muffins, lifts the tin foil cover, and smells. She sets them on her table and takes one out, bites into it. I wait for a reaction. "I just talked to the funeral home," she says, taking another bite. "They told me to come as soon as I'm ready. My meeting is with a guy named Conrad. Can you believe that? A funeral director named Conrad? I don't know, something about that seems creepy to me." She finishes off the muffin and reaches for another one. That's the response I'd hoped for.

"I'm sure Conrad is a very nice man," I say. "Maybe he goes by the name Con."

"Oh, that's better," she says. "I want a guy selling me coffins who goes by the name Con."

"Okay, maybe he goes by Rad. Radley?"

"As in Boo?" She grins. "You're not making me feel better, Finn."

"You know, he probably won't have anything to do with preparing your grandmother. He's just a director, right?"

Her smile fades. "I don't want to do this," she says. "I don't know if I can. I'm too young. Isn't there some rule that you have to be in your sixties to plan a funeral?"

"There should be."

"How did you do it?"

I'm actually embarrassed. I grab a muffin myself

and bite into it, hiding behind it. "How did I do what?"

"How did you plan your mother's funeral?"

I consider lying and making up something about how I stepped up to the plate and bit the bullet, or any of a dozen clichés that would make me look good. But I have to tell the truth. "Honestly, I didn't. I had relatives who did that."

"So you just had to show up?"

I don't say anything, and she just assumes that's true. What would she think if she knew I didn't even do that?

She bites into another muffin. Not hungry, huh? This is her third. "I'm seriously shaking like a leaf."

"Of course you are. It's a terrible thing to have to do. I'll be with you."

When she finishes off the rest of the muffins, she wipes her mouth. "Those were good. Did you realize I was eating the whole batch? Did you even get any?"

"I got what I wanted. If I'd known you were that hungry, I would have made two dozen."

"That's ridiculous," she says. "I wasn't hungry at all. They were just so good."

"You needed comfort food."

"I guess I did."

When she's ready and has worked up her resolve to go do this, she drives us to the funeral parlor. I'm uneasy because I'm so rarely in the passenger seat. But I try not to show it.

She gets us there in one piece, though some of her stops at intersections were iffy.

We step up to the door and it's mysteriously opened for us. The man called Conrad stands before us in a black suit with a gray pinstriped tie. There's not a single wrinkle anywhere. Has he been standing at the door since getting dressed? Or is there some special kind of funeral starch that prevents normal human creasing?

"How are you?" he says in a midhappy to sorrowful voice. That's a neat trick to pull off, I think. To straddle the line between happy and sad all day long, when he probably just feels indifference. After all, he does this all day, every day. It's not like he's mourning for each of his clients. But if he laughs or grins or cracks a joke—or wears color, God forbid— families could be deeply offended. I feel kind of sorry for the guy.

He takes us into a richly paneled room and sits behind his mahogany desk. It's exactly the way I pictured. "First, let me say how sorry I am to hear about your grandmother," he says in an oh-so-somber tone. "I know it was quite a shock. And on Christmas Day."

"Yeah, I'm really sorry about the timing," Sydney says. "I know you'd rather be spending time with your family."

"No, I assure you, your grandmother was not the only one. We have a lot of bookings over the holidays."

I look at Sydney and see how stricken she looks. "You mean lots of people die on Christmas? What is it about the holidays? The CDC needs to put a bulletin out. They need to warn people."

"It's always been this way," Conrad says. "My point in telling you that was to let you know that we're happy to help. Now, can you tell me what your budget is?"

Sydney looks distressed again. "What does it cost?"

"Well, that depends on several things. For instance, the cost of the casket you choose. We have various models. It also depends on where you have the service—here or at a church she attended.

Sometimes churches offer use of their sanctuaries for free to their members. And of course there are flowers, photography, and various other choices."

"I don't know the budget," Sydney says. "I don't have any cash lying around, and I sure wasn't expecting this. I don't know what Grammy had."

He takes notes, then looks back at her, and I get the feeling he's a disapproving teacher in a math class, hoping his student gets at least one problem right.

"So do you know who you would like to officiate at the funeral?"

Sydney frowns deeply and looks down at her lap. "Officiate?" she mumbles. "No, I don't have a—"

"I know who," I cut in. "Miss Callie's preacher. I've met him. She took me to visit him."

Sydney perks up. "Yes. We could ask him. That's right. It would make sense for her own preacher to officiate."

"Do you know his name?" Conrad asks.

I deflate again. "No, I don't remember his name. But I know the church. I can go back there and talk to him. We can go right after we leave here."

Conrad is trying to hide his frustration. "Do you know the name of the church?"

I squint up at the ceiling. "It was something-something Baptist. Big River, maybe. Is that a church?"

"Greater Rivers," he says, smiling broadly now as if he's forgotten he's supposed to be funereal. "Greater Rivers Baptist Church. The senior pastor there is Dr. Randall Seagrove."

"Huh," I say. "He didn't look like a doctor anybody. He was young . . . and single."

"They allow single men to get their doctorates." It's a joke, but no one laughs. Funny guy, that Conrad.

"So would you like to ask him yourself? He may not be aware that Mrs. Beecher has died. We're certainly willing to contact him, but sometimes the family prefers to talk to the pastor themselves. He can provide comfort in a time like this."

Sydney looks up at me, a question in her eyes.

"I'll go with you," I say quickly. "Since I've already met him and everything."

"Yes, okay. We'll go see him ourselves."

"Have him call me after you speak to him," Conrad says, "and we'll set a time for the service. Now, do you happen to know if Mrs. Beecher had a will?"

Sydney shakes her head. "No, I don't. She never told me."

"You might look through her things. See if you can find it. That might help you with planning, and possibly the budget. If you learn that you're the beneficiary, then perhaps you could use her money to pay for the funeral."

Sydney looks wan, and I pat her back and stroke it, trying to remind her that she's not alone. "Okay, I'll do that after we see the pastor."

"And we would like to have some photos. If you have any at all of her, we can blow them up and frame them to have at the funeral. We can even play a PowerPoint slideshow."

"Wow. There's no rest for the grieving, is there? I didn't know there was so much to do. Pictures, huh?"

I know her mind is drifting to where Callie might have pictures. Polaroids in a drawer somewhere?

"Also, we'll need clothes."

She sucks in a breath. "Of course. I should have brought them. I didn't think about that. I don't know why. I made a list last night of people to call and a million other things, but no clothes, which is ludicrous since she's been wearing the same thing since yesterday and it's probably not her favorite.

Should I buy her something new? Do I need to go shopping?"

I want to rescue her from her rambling, so I squeeze her trembling hand again. "I bet everybody forgets clothes, huh?"

"Yes. Practically everyone. You have plenty of time to get that to us. It doesn't have to be new." Conrad rises to his feet. "Now, if you'd like to join me in the next room, we can look at the various choices of caskets."

Sydney doesn't move. "Do I . . . have to do it now?"

"It would be helpful," Conrad says. "At the very least I can give you several options, and you can go home and think about it and let me know sometime today."

Her hand is sweating, but it's ice cold. We finally get up and follow him into the room next door. It's a warehouse room full of every model of caskets, from bronze to gold to deep rich mahogany, to the basic boxes with hinges that look like they could be plastic. I stay very quiet, not sure what would make Sydney feel better. She's wavering now, as if she's going to pass out.

"Conrad," I ask, "do you happen to have any brochures with all the choices?"

"Yes, of course we do." He goes and pulls one out of a rack and hands it to Sydney. "Why don't you make a choice and call us back? We can take your payment over the phone if it's on a credit card. Otherwise you can come by and pay with a check."

"Are the prices on here?" I ask, because I know she'll want to know.

"Yes, they're in a chart at the back."

"Okay, we'll be in touch." I take her elbow, but she's just staring in front of her. "Want to go now?"

She nods, distracted, and lets me escort her down the hall and back to the car, and it isn't until I pull out of the parking lot that she takes a deep breath. "I think I'm gonna faint."

"Then you should breathe," I say, taking her hand. "Just take a deep breath and let it out slowly."

She does as I say . . . breathes in . . . then out. "I don't want to say good-bye to my grandmother. I'm not ready. I haven't known her long enough."

"I know," I say. "It always seems too soon." My mind wanders back to my mother, when I finally went to her grave about two weeks too late. I sat on the grass and wept like a baby, hating myself for letting her down.

"Where are we going?" Sydney asks.

"To the church," I remind her. "To talk to the hot Dr. Seagrove. He was one of Callie's picks for you."

She smirks. "I wish you hadn't told me that."

"But he seemed to like her a lot, so it shouldn't be a terrible experience. You might even get a date out of it."

Laughter pushes through her mood. "Stop, okay? I don't want you to make me laugh."

"Sorry. I just want you to feel better, and to know that this isn't going to be as hard as you think."

"I guess I can't put it off." Tears rush to her eyes, and I pull out a Kleenex and hand it to her. She dabs at her eyes.

We get to the church, and I park. Sydney doesn't move to get out. "Do you think we should have made an appointment? Maybe I should've called first."

"I'm sure it's okay. When I took Callie, she walked right in. He was happy to see her."

"But it's the day after Christmas."

"People work the day after Christmas."

I get out and walk around to her door. She gets

out but just stands there for a moment, looking toward the building. "You can lean on me for support," I say. "No one expects you to be strong today."

"But I want to be strong," she says. "I don't want to be a wilting rose. I'm not like that. I don't want you to think—"

I put my arm around her. "Sydney, your being upset over your grandmother's death is not weak. Trust me, I know weak."

We go in, and I lead her to the office. The secretary smiles, and it seems genuine. "Is Dr. Seagrove in?"

"Yes, he is. Can I tell him who's here?"

"Callie Beecher's granddaughter," Sydney says.

"Oh, sure. We love Miss Callie. She is such a sweetie. Always makes us laugh."

The secretary gets to the door of the pastor's office, but before opening it she looks back at Sydney. "I hope you haven't come to give us bad news about her."

Sydney's eyes glisten. "Grammy passed away yesterday. In her sleep."

The secretary's hand goes to her heart. "On Christmas Day? Oh, honey!" She comes back and hugs Sydney. "Oh, darlin', I'm so sorry."

"Thank you," Sydney says.

The secretary looks shaken as she knocks on the pastor's door and steps inside to whisper to him. When she comes back and opens the door wider, Dr. Seagrove is coming around the desk, a serious look on his face. "You're Callie's granddaughter? I've heard lots about you."

"I bet you have," she says. "I'm sorry about that, Dr. . . ."

"Please, call me Randy," he says. "And what's your name?"

"Sydney. And this is Finn."

"Yes, I remember you, Finn. So she passed away yesterday?"

The words *passed away* have always baffled me. I don't understand why people find it so hard to use the word *died* about their loved ones. I use *passed away* myself when I talk about my mother's death.

We make small talk for a few minutes, then Sydney asks if he will officiate at the funeral. "Of course I will. And I'll let her church family know. A lot of our members will want to come pay Callie their respects. She was a very cherished member of our congregation until she was homebound. But now that we're talking about her funeral, there's some stuff I need to tell you." He goes to open a cabinet drawer, digs to the back of it, and pulls out a shoebox.

"You know, it's funny. Miss Callie always had strange requests, and she sometimes had us jump through hoops. She gave us all a lot of chuckles. But one day a few weeks ago, she came in here with a tape recorder and insisted on recording something in front of me. She said that when she died she wanted me to get this to you. She even left a cassette player in this box because she felt sure you wouldn't have one to play it on."

"A tape?" Sydney asks. "For me?"

"It's not very long," Seagrove says. "At the time I thought she was being a little melodramatic. But she insisted you hear this from her."

He plugs in the tape recorder and puts the cassette in. He presses Play and sits back. We hear Callie's cheerful voice, as if she's right here with us. "Pastor, I've told you about my lovely grand-daughter, Sydney," she says. "You know, she isn't married. I would love for you to meet her. You can't stay single forever."

Sydney covers her face, horrified. I laugh with the pastor, picturing Callie shaking her finger at him.

"I guess you're right," he tells Callie with a chuckle.

"So when you're ready, I would like to introduce you. But if you don't meet her before I die . . ."

"You're going to live forever, Miss Callie," he says. "We all know that."

"I'll live *somewhere* forever," she says. "I'll be with Jesus. And that's why I really don't care about this . . . this body of mine."

"What do you mean, Miss Callie?" His voice has lost its humorous edge.

There's a short pause, then she says, "This part is for Sydney." Her tone changes then and gets slightly louder, as if she's leaning toward the microphone. "Honey, I know you won't want this, but I want my body donated to science."

Sydney sucks in a breath. "No!"

"Science?" the pastor asks on the tape. "Why?"

"Because I've never been a modest woman," she says. "I'm not self-conscious like that. I don't care if after I die people are staring at my . . . Oh, what do they call it? Cadaver? Or if they're using a microscope to see things. They have to do research on somebody, don't they?"

"Well, yes, I guess they do."

"My daughter, Sydney's mother, she died when Sydney was so small. Gloria had her whole life before her. They just didn't know enough about the cancer she had. If someone had donated their body, maybe my girl could have been cured. Now I might have some things inside me that people might want to see and study." She gives a slight giggle. "People have always told me I'm one of a kind."

The pastor chuckles, but Sydney is still in shock. I follow her lead.

"I want to be useful for as long as I can," Callie says.

"Grammy!" Sydney whispers.

The pastor's voice on the tape is full of empathy. "That makes perfect sense, Miss Callie. So do you have any particular place you want your body donated?"

"I'm thinking the medical college is as good as any. But honestly, I'm not particular. Just wherever my Sydney thinks is the best place. Wherever I can be most useful."

Sydney leans across the desk and stops the tape.

"Wait. So . . . she didn't want a casket? Or any funeral at all?"

"You can still have a funeral," Pastor Seagrove says. "In fact, try and stop us. We have to celebrate Miss Callie."

Sydney looks faint again. "I don't know if I can donate her body."

"Of course you can. It's what she wanted. We can do the funeral up big."

"But they could already be embalming her."

"I doubt it. Not until they've gotten signatures. I can call the funeral parlor as soon as we're done here and let them know."

Swallowing, Sydney presses Play again.

Miss Callie's voice starts back up. "You know, Sydney, that it won't really be me in that body. Just a shell. I know people say that all the time, but I want you to know it's true. I'll be tickled to be with Jesus. We'll be catching up. Well, I will. He knows all about me already, but I want to know every little thing that he's done since he left this earth. I'm going to ask lots of questions."

Seagrove laughs as if he can see it. "Oh, I know you are."

"It'll be so glorious. When I was a girl I went to camp, and we had a mountaintop experience every day. And then I came home and things got a little dull." She chuckles again, and her voice lowers so that I picture the pastor leaning in. "I can just imagine heaven being a mountaintop experience every day . . . every hour, just as much as you can stand, till your heart just can't hold anymore."

"I'm sure that's how it is," her pastor assures her.

My eyes are full, and I look at Sydney. She's not even trying to hide her tears now. And neither am I.

CHAPTER 27

Finn

I accompany Sydney back to Callie's house, and both of us walk through it in silence, looking around the place where we celebrated yesterday. The absence of the old woman is stark and brutal. We search the places where Callie might have put her will, opening drawers, thumbing through papers.

Finally, Sydney locates it in a cabinet in Callie's bedroom. She sits on Callie's bed and unfolds the document.

I wait inside the doorway, leaning against the dresser, giving her time and space to figure it out.

After a few minutes, she blots her eyes and looks up at me.

"She left me everything. The house, the bank account, everything. Oh, and her Bible. She made a special note that I was to get her Bible. It was like she set it apart from all the other stuff, like it was the most valuable thing she had."

I glance around the room and see it sitting on Callie's bed table. I lift it reverently and take it to Sydney. I sit down on the bed next to her as she opens it.

"Look. She wrote in it. All these notes."

"Now you'll have to read it," I say.

Tears rush to her eyes again. "Yeah, I'll do that." She finds a Post-it note sticking on a page at the back, and she opens the Bible there, at Revelation 21. Callie's notes and exclamations fill the ample margins.

"Read it," I whisper.

"It's about heaven," Sydney says. She starts to read, and I close my eyes and try to imagine what the words mean. Heaven is a place I never thought much about, a place I just hoped existed. I don't understand all of what I hear, but deep in my soul

I hear the promise of no more tears or death or mourning or pain. She reads of the precious stones, the gates of pearl, and the illumination that's not set off by the sun because there's no need of one.

By the time Sydney comes to the end, I realize I'm holding my breath. I let it out and look at the words as her finger moves under them. "The Spirit and the bride say, 'Come.' And let the one who hears say, 'Come.' And let the one who is thirsty come; let the one who wishes take the water of life without cost." She looks up at me, her eyes packed full of the same kind of things I'm thinking. I nod for her to go on. She reads more, then comes to a point that hitches my heart. "He who testifies to these things says, 'Yes, I am coming quickly.' Amen. Come, Lord Jesus."

We're quiet for a long moment as we stare at those words. "Look," I say finally, pointing to Callie's note on the side of the page.

She's written, "I'm coming home!! Can't wait to see it!"

Sydney covers her mouth and dissolves. "It's like she really was excited to go."

"If you believe what she believed, I guess it would

only stand to reason that you would be excited to get there."

We take a moment to read Callie's small hand-written comments in the margins of the heaven chapters. I put my arm around Sydney as she thumbs through. It's as if she's sitting here with us, showing us things that thrill her.

"What a gift," I say when Sydney closes the book and holds it to her heart.

"Yeah," she says. "I think she had something there. It did need to be set apart. Grammy thought of everything."

"I hope this gives you a little more peace," I say. "It sure does me."

I can see that her smile is genuine. "It does. It's almost like Grammy was looking out for me even in death. Trying to make me feel better. Making me understand where she is." She gets up and goes to Callie's dresser and picks up her hairbrush. "It's just that she was such a special lady. And now we're going to have a funeral that's more of a memorial service, and I doubt that many people will come. At her age, all of her friends must have died before her. What if nobody comes but the preacher?"

"I'll be there," I say. "And I can guarantee you there'll be others."

When I leave her there a little while later, I'm determined to make my promise come true. I'm going to get a crowd there for Callie. I'll go to every person she dragged me to, everyone I know who knows her. I won't take no for an answer.

Callie Beecher is going to draw a crowd.

CHAPTER 28

Finn

First, I head to the dry cleaners, not sure if it'll even be open today, the day after Christmas. But when I get there, their Open sign is lit up.

"May I help you?" the girl at the counter asks.

"Can I see the manager, please?"

She knocks on the door where Callie went to talk to him just days ago. It seems like so long ago now.

The manager steps out and reaches across the counter to shake my hand. "Hey. Roger Jenkins," he says.

"Finn Parrish. I brought Callie Beecher here to talk to you the other day."

"Yeah, we love Miss Callie," he says. "We've been doing business with her for years. Not so much lately, but we still like seeing her now and then."

"Well, I'm afraid I have bad news. Callie passed away yesterday in her sleep."

He gives the same old response. "On Christmas Day?"

"That's right," I say. "I'm sorry to bring the news, but I wanted to let you know that the funeral is going to be at ten o'clock the day after tomorrow at the Greater Rivers Baptist Church. I wondered if you'd come."

"Of course I'll be there."

"I want to make sure people come," I say in case he's just blowing smoke. "She has a granddaughter who cares a lot about her. I don't want it to be one of those funerals. You know, the kind where only a handful of people are there. That would be sad." I know I'm putting a guilt trip on him, twisting his arm, but I really don't care. What I care about is Sydney and how she feels tomorrow.

"Sure, yes, I'll be there. I loved Miss Callie. We're going to miss her."

I thank him and ask him to let the rest of the

staff know, and to invite them to come. As I step to the door and push it open, he says, "Mr. Parrish?"

I look back.

"Now that I think about it, it's kind of appropriate, don't you think? Her passing away on Christmas Day? I think she would've liked that. That day was always real important to her."

"Yeah, it was. And I can tell you she had a real good Christmas before it happened."

"That's good," he says. "She deserved that."

I walk back out to the car and head to the bank where Callie talked to the branch manager. I do the same with him—force his agreement to show up at the funeral. Then I go to Macy's, where she struck up a conversation with the girl behind the counter when she bought those plaid towels.

I tell the girl about Callie, and even though she doesn't know the name, she remembers her. "Look, I know this is a crazy request," I say. "But Callie was a real special woman. And it means a lot to her granddaughter to give her a proper funeral. It would just be really great if you could come and bring some friends. I just want people to be there, you know?"

"Sure," she says. "I can pack a pew."

I go back to the church. The pastor is out right now, but I talk to the secretary. "I was here this morning with Callie Beecher's granddaughter?"

"Yes, darlin'," she says. "Is there anything I can do?"

"Yes, as a matter of fact," I say. "Would you make sure that everyone knows about Callie? If there's an email list or people you could contact? The choir or the Sunday School?"

"Absolutely," she says. "I'll let everybody know, I promise. We have a massive grapevine here. Don't worry, we'll turn out for our precious Callie."

Sitting behind the steering wheel, I try to think where else I can find people who might care about Callie. Her neighborhood! Of course. I drive there, park in her driveway, and walk from door to door up and down her block. Only half of them are home, but those who are know who Callie is and thank me for telling them about the funeral.

When I get back to my car, I feel a sense of sadness that there isn't more I can do. I don't know who else to invite. As I drive home, I pray that God will work it out for Sydney. This whole praying thing gets easier every time I do it. I feel like I'm getting to know Callie's Jesus a little better, even though I'm doing all the talking. But he speaks volumes in the way he listens.

CHAPTER 29

Sydney

The funeral home asked for some pictures to enlarge for the funeral, so I go to Grammy's house and get her boxes of photos and picture albums. I guess they're mine now.

I look around at all her stuff and wonder how I'm going to sort through eighty years of possessions. There's so much of her here. I missed so much of her life, and I won't recognize most of it.

I'll have to figure that out later.

Back home, I spread the pictures out on my dining room table and page through the albums. There are faded black-and-white photos of Grammy when she was a young woman. I turn to a page where she's holding a baby dressed in a frilly lace dress, all in white, with a sweet little bonnet. I look more closely and realize it's my mom.

She's laughing, and her bottom two teeth are showing. Grammy is grinning with pride.

I go from picture to picture, watching my mother grow up and Grammy grow older. Why have I never seen these before?

I pull out a few of the pictures and set them aside on the table. Soon I have so many that I know I'll have to do a PowerPoint slide show so the few mourners at the funeral can see her.

Grammy's smile is even broader in the pictures where she's holding me as a baby. It feels self-indulgent to pull all of those out for the PowerPoint. But this is the life I had before my first memories. The life I lost when my mother died and my father was left alone with me. Somehow these photos comfort me.

Then I realize Grammy never showed me these because I so rarely sat down with her. I was always in triage mode, seeing to her needs, but not spending time with her. Not listening. Not seeing.

I miss her voice, and her embarrassing proclamations, and her way of thinking. I miss her wrinkled face and her soft touch. She was so proud of me. No matter how often I thought I'd let her down, I could do no wrong in her eyes.

I turn from the pictures and go to my back window, looking out on my yard. It was beautiful when I bought the house, with rosebushes and a little fishpond. I have a guy who mows and weeds, but I haven't walked out there in months. What a waste.

I step out onto the patio now. The Adirondack chair I bought with the house is covered with old pollen, but I drop into it anyway and look up to the dusky sky.

"I'm so sorry I missed all that," I whisper. "I missed everything she said. Everything she showed me. I want to honor her now, even though it's too late. I want to do what I should have done before."

I can't believe I'm talking to God again, whom I've rarely talked to before. But Grammy prayed as if God was sitting right beside her, as if there was no difference between that and any other kind of conversation. And as I attempt the same thing, I can tell that God takes notice.

A while later, Finn stops by to bring food as I'm trying to figure out what to wear to the funeral.

"Would you give me your opinion on something?" I ask him. "I have to decide what to wear tomorrow."

"Sure. Do I get a fashion show?"

"No, but I'll bring the outfits out here." I run into the bedroom and grab my choices, realizing I have way too much black in my wardrobe. I take them to the living room and lay them over the back of the couch. I pick up the first one—a business suit with a short jacket and a midcalf skirt.

"Nope," he says. "Next."

I gape at him, surprised. "Really? I thought you would be one of those guys who pretends to like everything."

"Have you met me?"

I laugh. "Okay, what about this one? It has a longer jacket, and it has some blue in it."

"Next."

"Wow. Okay, this one?"

"Don't you have anything other than suits? Just regular dresses?"

"I mostly buy suits for work."

He drops into the easy chair next to the couch. "That's what gets me. Why do women in professional positions like yours have to dress in suits?"

"Because we have to try harder."

"You don't. I bet you're a great lawyer."

I sigh. "It's just the way it's done. We wear jackets. Heels. We have to look professional."

"So that explains the opiate epidemic. Women who have to clomp around in heels. The men don't wear heels. Why do women have to?"

I can't believe Finn is making me have this conversation. "Because it looks more dressy. But you know, I've always thought that a man must have invented high heels. No one who had to wear those things would ever inflict that on the rest of her gender."

"Then stop wearing them."

"But they're cuter than flats."

"Oh, so you do want to look cute? Not like a man?"

"In some ways, yes."

"Sydney, you have the market cornered on cute. You don't need to walk on stilettos."

I'm touched, but I pretend I didn't hear it. "So

I'll wear lower heels to the funeral. But seriously, you don't like any of these outfits?"

"No."

Sighing, I stack them up and carry them back to my room, and go through my closet to pull out the few real dresses I have. I take them out and find Finn in the kitchen checking the food in my fridge. "These aren't black. I don't know if I can wear any of them."

"Why should you wear black?"

"Because I'm sad."

"But Callie is happy, right? She's celebrating. Walking and running and working the crowd. I bet *she's* wearing color."

"I think she's probably wearing one of those white robes we read about in her Bible."

"So wear white."

"Are you crazy? You don't wear white to a funeral."

He leans toward me across the kitchen island. "You may have noticed this about me, but I'm not big on style."

"I know," I say. "You want me to be comfortable. But I can't wear a T-shirt and yoga pants."

He comes back into the living room and looks at

the choices, considering them more carefully. "This one," he says. "I like the purple."

I incline my head and consider it. It's a dark purple, not bright, so maybe it would be appropriate enough. I take it and hold it up to me.

"Yep, that's it." He grins. "Look at those eyes."

I'm not sure how he's done it, but he's made me feel beautiful and happy rather than awkward and sad. "Okay, I'll wear this. Thank you."

He won't let me lift a finger as he brings lasagna to the table and serves me. I savor the taste. "This is fantastic. You really are good."

"Thanks."

"You should be cooking for a living. Not that you're not a great cab driver. You are. But this . . . this is a real gift."

He smiles, and as he takes a bite, I realize he enjoys what he cooks as much as I do.

He's just one more thing to be grateful for.

CHAPTER 30

Finn

I'm cleaning the dishes in Sydney's kitchen when she asks if I want to see the pictures she's going to use for the PowerPoint slide show for the funeral.

I dry my hands and go sit beside her, studying each one.

"Did you make one of these when your mother died?" she asks.

I shake my head no.

"Did you have framed pictures?"

I stare at a picture of Callie holding baby Sydney and clear my throat. She thinks I'm a nice guy. Maybe it's time to tell her the truth.

"Sydney, I've let you assume something about me without setting you straight."

"What?"

"About my mother. See . . . I loved my mom. But I was a jerk when she died."

"Well, it's a hard thing. People react differently."

I shift in my seat. "No, I mean . . . Maybe *jerk* isn't the right word. Maybe *coward* is more accurate."

I have her full attention now. I wish I didn't have to go on, that I could rewrite that chapter of my life so it doesn't sound so bad.

"I went to see her in the hospital when she was dying, and . . . when I saw her lying there with all the tubes and wires . . . I just left. I didn't even go in."

She looks at me for a long moment, and I know what's going through her mind. *He's inadequate, he's cold, he's nothing but some cab driver who didn't feel empathy even for his own mother.*

But she doesn't say anything like that. She surprises me by touching my hand. "Okay."

"There's more." I draw in a ragged breath and meet her eyes. "I didn't show up for the funeral."

She blinks. "Oh."

"I was her only child, and I didn't go." I rub the sweat forming over my lip. "You know, now that I think about it, *jerk* probably does cover it."

She lets go of my hand. "No, I think *coward* was good."

It takes me a minute to realize she's not serious. She takes my hand again and leans toward me. "Finn, you're not a coward now."

Tears pushing to my eyes horrify me, and when she hugs me I'm glad she can't see them.

I don't want to leave, so I watch her cues and she seems to want me to stay. After I've cleaned up the dishes, I join her on the couch, watching some romantic comedy that I couldn't care less about. I just want her to feel content.

After a while, she lays her head on my shoulder, and I take that as a cue that I can put my arm around her. Before I know it, she's sound asleep. I wonder if she's slept at all in the last few days.

I could sit here with her all night, basking in the warmth that defines her. I could be here when she wakes up. But will she want me here in the light of a fresh morning?

What if she wakes up and thinks I'm the most

presumptuous idiot she has ever shared time with? What if she remembers she's out of my league, that I'm nothing but the cab driver, that I wasn't there for my own mom?

Reminders of my inadequacy will run like a loop through her mind. Sure, I'm good when she's stunned by a death and doesn't want to be alone. But given a choice, given a comparison with almost any other guy, I'll come up lacking.

I don't know what I was thinking to let myself be this familiar with her.

I gently slide out from under her head and move a pillow there. I find a throw over a chair and cover her with it.

Then I grab her phone, which doesn't require a passcode, and I set an alarm for the morning so she won't oversleep. I set it on the coffee table next to her. I text her that I'll see her at the funeral. Then I press the shadow of a kiss on her cheek just before I leave.

CHAPTER 31

Finn

The main floor of the sanctuary of Callie's church is filling up. There's her banker coming in with some others, and just before it starts, the dry cleaner slips in. Several of the neighbors I visited scatter throughout the room. And her church turns out in a way I never would have expected.

I'm surprised by the group I see crowding through the doorway. My dispatcher, LuAnn, trots in, wearing stretchy black pants too tight for her not-so-skinny hips, and her teased flip-up hairdo and cat's-eye glasses. She's followed by Lamar, with his Duck Dynasty beard, and at least a dozen other taxi drivers wearing their usual jeans and T-shirts. It has to be a big day for Uber.

I get their attention, and they squeeze into the pew next to me.

"How ya doing, Finn?" LuAnn says.

"Good. How'd you get all these guys here?"

She grins. "I told them she was your mama."

I groan. "LuAnn, you're kidding."

"Hush now," she whispers. "They think they're doing something nice."

I make room as the ragtag team of drivers scoot past me, each shaking my hand and offering awkward condolences.

The more I think about it, the funnier it gets. Still, I'm touched that they would come. You wouldn't get a bunch of Uber drivers here.

By the time the pastor takes his seat on the stage, there's a respectable crowd gathered to pay their respects to Callie. Her body has already been donated to the local medical college, but there are flowers and sprays that people have sent. I want to kick myself. I should have sent some. Why didn't I think of that?

I'm beating myself up about it when Conrad and

another funeral guy go to the front and motion for us all to stand. Then the door opens, and Sydney walks in, followed by some strangers I assume are relatives. I wonder if she even knows them. I watch as her gaze sweeps the crowd, and she smiles with soft surprise at the number of people. She takes her seat on the front row. The rest of the relatives file into the row behind her. I don't like her sitting there alone, but I can't very well walk up there like I'm somebody.

I'm still just the cab driver.

"Why aren't you up there?" Squint-Eyed Bill asks me as the pastor walks to the stage.

"I don't like people staring at me," I explain. He's satisfied with that.

A woman goes up onto the stage and sings "I'll Fly Away," and Callie's church friends begin to clap like they're at a hoedown. I'm not sure it's appropriate for a funeral. But when the pastor gets up, he tells us why.

"That was Miss Callie's favorite song," he says. "And every time she heard it, she would clap a little off rhythm, until the whole church was clapping along. I never hear that song without thinking of her.

"Those of you who knew Miss Callie have stories of your own, but I want to share some of the Callieisms that I witnessed personally," he says. "She was always funny and blunt, but as she got older, she kind of lost her filter. Like the time she told a guy whose pants were sagging that nobody wanted to see his patootie."

The crowd laughs, and I smile, too.

"Yes, she really said *patootie*. She asked him how he could even walk with his pants falling down. He mumbled something about it being comfortable, and she said, 'It's sure not comfortable for those of us who have to see it.'"

The audience cracks up, and I see that Sydney is laughing, too.

"Back when my dad was the pastor here, Miss Callie had the youth group over for tea to talk to us about a mission project. After the tea, she revealed that the mission project was in her yard. Before we knew it, she had us weeding her garden and planting flowers. She had a way of getting you to do what she wanted. You didn't say no to Miss Callie. And if she told you to pull up your pants, you did."

We laugh our way through the ceremony, and

somehow that makes the sorrow seem a little more manageable. When the pastor lists the things Callie did for the church over the years and reads her Post-it note scripture about heaven, I find a sense of peace falling over me.

I'm glad I knew Callie and got caught up in the tornado of her intentions. I'm glad she entangled me in her schemes. I'm honored to have been there with Sydney at the end.

And I'm glad I had the chance to meet the God she trusted in. I hope someday I can trust him like that, too.

CHAPTER 32

Finn

There's quite a group in the fellowship hall by the time I make my way through the crowd. The large dining hall is flanked by a kitchen, where some of Callie's churchmates have fixed lunch. They stand in a line behind a series of tables, serving food as mourners come through with trays.

Sydney isn't eating. I see her across the room, shaking hands and collecting condolences. She looks more relaxed than she has at any time during this process. Maybe the laughter during the service steadied her.

I'm glad. I can't stand to think of her trapped in sadness.

I make my way toward her, staying on the outskirts, trying not to look like I'm waiting for her.

A cute brunette moves gracefully in front of me. "I have to say this is the best-looking funeral crowd I've ever seen," she says. She looks like another lawyer. She's wearing a black suit with a white blouse and the trademark black pumps.

"You think so?" I ask.

"Yeah. I'm Joanie," she says.

I shake her hand. "Hi, Joanie. How did you know Callie?"

"Oh, I didn't. I work with her granddaughter. Well . . . worked, until Christmas Day. Imagine my surprise when I came in yesterday and got her cases dumped on me."

"Yeah, bad day to lose your job. But she shouldn't have been having to work that day."

She takes a sip of her iced tea and grins up at me. "So how did you know Miss Callie?"

I smile. "I was her driver."

Her warmth seems to cool a bit. "Seriously?"

"Yep. I drive a cab."

"Oh, you're the one who took her to the doctor?"

I'm surprised Sydney has admitted that. "Yeah, among other places."

"Sydney mentioned that. She felt horrible that she couldn't do it. But it was brutal at work. Seriously brutal."

It sounds as if they're friends, so I let my guard down a little. "So did you get stuck with her Burger King crasher case?"

"Yes. Yes, I did. I could kill her. I can't believe she survived the staff cuts and then let this happen. I know it was Christmas, but if she could have just hung on."

I bristle a little. "Her grandmother was dying."

All traces of her flirty smile are gone now. "I know, but she needs a job. It's her lifelong dream."

"Maybe it's your lifelong dream to work for a group of people who won't let you have Christmas Day off when your grandmother is dying, all because your drunk client ran into an electrical pole. I don't think it's hers."

She seems offended and mutters something about having to talk to someone. She moves on to the banker who's hovering near Sydney.

I feel bad about insulting her. She did care enough to come, after all.

I go to the drink table and pour myself an iced tea. I'm closer to Sydney now, and I listen as Callie's dry cleaner takes Sydney's hand. "Your grandmother tried to fix me up with you," he says. "I never paid attention. But when I saw you today, I realized she was onto something."

Sydney laughs, and her cheeks blush. "Well, I'm sorry about all that. I never asked her to do it."

"I thought maybe we could have dinner sometime. You know, in her honor."

Her gaze snaps up to mine, and I turn away. I move out of the crowd so she can feel free to give her number out to as many of Callie's picks as she wants. She seems in her element, and she looks lovely. I should have let her wear the first man-suit she picked out last night. What was I thinking, talking her into a purple that highlights the blue in her eyes?

But why shouldn't she show all those losers what they've been missing? What made me think that she would settle for the only one who came for Christmas? Just because she seems perfect for me doesn't mean I'm perfect for her.

I'm the cab driver. I'm Callie's last resort, not her first choice for Sydney. Sydney turned to me in a vulnerable moment, but really, can I hold her to that? Can I expect any of it to continue after this awful time is over?

Why on earth would she ever choose someone like me?

After a while, the crowd begins to thin. Sydney makes her way to me.

"Hey," she says. "Did you eat?"

"Not hungry," I say. "You?"

"Not really. Maybe later."

I try to keep things light. "Callie would have been thrilled with all these single men here."

She laughs and looks back toward the people. "Yeah, that's kind of mortifying. Finn, I know what you did. Almost all these people came because of you. I really appreciate it."

I shrug. "They just needed to be told."

"But still. Everything you've done . . . I don't know what I would have done without you. I think God sent you when both Grammy and I needed a friend."

"Wow," I say. "That's nice . . . to think of it that way."

"It's true. Thank you for everything."

I look down at her for a moment, and I can't escape the sense that she's dismissing me.

Pastor Seagrove touches her shoulder, pulling her away from me. He says something that makes her laugh.

Callie would love the thought of her with him.

I step away, then turn and head to the exit. I look back before I leave. Sydney's eyes are bright, looking up into the pastor's face as he waxes humorous about something.

I make my way out to my cab and sit in it for a minute with the engine idling. I roll down the window, letting the cold wind whip through. This time with Callie hasn't been wasted. My life is changed from knowing her. It's changed for knowing Sydney. It's changed for brushing against Jesus, who orchestrated a do-over for me, even if it wasn't with my own mother.

I'm awake now, after years of being asleep. I'll find a way to stretch my life back into place. And I'll pray for what's best for Sydney. I'll root for her. I'll be her biggest fan. Maybe even her friend.

But why is it so hard to leave this place? I put

the car in reverse and back out of my space, then drive through the parking lot maze toward the exit.

"Finn!"

I stop when I hear my name, and I look in my rearview mirror. Sydney is running toward me, and suddenly, with certainty, I know Callie's God is real.

She throws open my passenger door and slides inside. "Finn . . . thank goodness you didn't leave. I needed to tell you . . . I wanted to say . . ." She's trying to catch her breath.

"You okay?" I ask.

"Yes." She leans across the console and lays one on me. A kiss, that is. She kisses me.

It's as if the clouds break on a hurricane day, as if the sun comes out to dry up the floods. It's as if there are four rainbows encircling me, as if it's early Christmas Day.

When she pulls back, I scramble for words. "I'm thinking of becoming a chef again."

She squints at me. "That's what you were thinking about while we were kissing?"

I realize it's ludicrous. "I just want you to know I'm not going to keep coasting."

She strokes my jaw and laughs aloud. "And I'm going to coast a little more. That okay with you?"

"Anything you do is okay with me." I kiss her again, keenly aware that God is answering my prayer for Sydney. Maybe I really *am* what's best for her. When we finally break again, I draw in a deep breath. "Do you want me to go back in with you?"

"No," she says. "Just drive."

"You don't want to go back in there? There are bankers and ministers and business owners lurking in hopes of getting your phone number."

Sydney shakes her head. "Too late now. Grammy died when her work was done."

I couldn't agree more. I can't get the stupid smile off my face as I drive. That plucky lady knew exactly what she was doing.

Author Note

It's often hard for me to be happy at Christmas. I always have great expectations about how happy my family will be as we come together and how much each person will love what I get them. I work myself to death, buying multiple gifts for every member of my family, decorating and wrapping, until every ounce of joy just drains right out of me.

I've recently been studying the science of happiness through a course Yale University is offering to the public. It's been fascinating and enlightening. I've learned that half of our happiness quotient is determined by genetics, and ten percent is determined by circumstances. But a full forty percent is made up of our thoughts and our actions, and those are completely within our control. The professor who teaches the course, Laura Santos, uses research to point out several clear paths to happiness. I've been most surprised to realize that, though she may not be aware of it, the actions and thoughts she suggests for "rewiring" our brains are biblical principles.

Spending time keeping a gratitude journal—so that you can dwell on those things you're grateful for—will help "rewire" the brain. The brain doesn't maintain a state of delight for very long, and you get used to the things that make you happy, which fools you into thinking you're no longer happy. Studies suggest taking time to think about what life would be like without those things or people you're grateful for. Imagine life without them. That will bring back the brief surge of joy you experienced when you got those things. The more you think about your gratitude for specific things or people, the happier you become.

The same is not true when you dwell on things that annoy you, because that makes you more miserable. (This is a wake-up call for those of us who listen to the news all day. It makes us dwell on our annoyances and fears instead of the things we're grateful for.)

It also turns out that experiences make us happier than material things, because of that frustrating feature of our brains that makes us grow bored. An experience is a onetime thing that gives us a surge of joy, and then it ends. We don't have time to get bored with it. A new car that we love sticks around for a while, so even if it causes great joy at the beginning, that joy wanes and we don't think we like it as much. If we realize that our brains do this, we can counteract it and reset the joy. If we don't realize it, we will complain and be disappointed and convince ourselves that we need another new purchase to make us happy.

This principle applies to relationships, too. We don't stay in the honeymoon phase for long. Our brains adjust to our joy with each other, and we interpret that as boredom, even though nothing has changed except for the way our brains perceive things. How many marriages and relationships have been wrecked due to our belief that the grass is greener on the other side? That very idea is a trick our minds play on us.

I've been most surprised that the scientific research into what actually leads to happiness points to a few very clear paths. In addition to gratitude, they include kindness to others, social connections, meditation, and goal setting.

As I've been watching these videos, I've felt a strange sense of déjà vu. I've heard all of this before. But where? Oh yes. I've read it in the Bible. The Yale University psychology department may not be aware that this research has proven very clear biblical principles, but it has. The Bible, written two thousand to four thousand years ago, doesn't tell us the scientific reasons behind these principles. And the research doesn't tell us the spiritual reasons behind them.

But what scientists have concluded as they've reinvented the wheel—or at least sought to explain how the wheel works—are sound ways to live our lives. God's Word links gratitude and peace in Philippians 4:6–7 and Colossians 3:15. On kindness, we're told to put others before ourselves. "Do unto others as you would have them do unto you." We're told that if you're asked for a shirt, give your coat. If you're asked to carry something one mile, carry it two. We're told not to keep a record of wrongs, but to consider how to stimulate one another with love and good deeds. And we're promised that "the fruit of the Spirit is love, joy, peace, patience, kindness, goodness, faithfulness, gentleness, self-control" (Galatians 5:22–23).

Studies suggest meditation as one of the paths to happiness. We call that prayer in Christendom. We're told, "Devote yourselves to prayer, keeping alert in it with an attitude of thanksgiving" (Colossians 4:2). It's not a new concept that taking time to quietly focus on things outside ourselves is good for our souls.

And who has better social connections than church members? We're told not to forsake our assembling together, because God knows we gain encouragement, support, and happiness from those connections with others.

As for goal setting, the apostle Paul tells us to "press on toward the goal for the prize of the upward call of God in Christ Jesus" (Philippians 3:14). Christians have much to look forward to, and our lives have purpose even when we're suffering.

I've known all this for years, but it took seeing

a scientific approach for me to remember that God has already given us every tool we need to be happy. And now, as Christmas draws near, I'm committed to focusing on the things that truly will bring me happiness. I'm not going to lose myself in the things that can't possibly provide sustained joy, but in the *experiences* that bring memories we can relive time and time again. I'm going to do that by implementing the principles I learned in the happiness studies, and those God has taught me over many years of reading his Word.

"Finally, brethren, whatever is true, whatever is honorable, whatever is right, whatever is pure, whatever is lovely, whatever is of good repute, if there is any excellence and if anything worthy of praise, dwell on these things" (Philippians 4:8).

Join me in this, and celebrate Jesus's birthday with true joy this year.

Merry Christmas!
Terri

Acknowledgments

One day a few years ago, I had a doctor's appointment at a local hospital. I was sitting in a huge waiting room where a couple hundred others were waiting, when I saw a man wheel an old woman in. He checked her in at the desk, where he had a significant wait to get to the front of the line. During that time, the woman said some embarrassing things very loudly and made all of us laugh. A few minutes later, the man wheeled the woman toward where I was sitting and locked her wheelchair right next to me. It was clear she had dementia, so when he handed her a business card and said, "Call me when you're done," I looked up at him and said, "You're not leaving her here alone, are you?"

The man looked at me and said, "Lady, I'm just the cab driver."

That planted the seed for this book, and the old woman who amused me for the next half hour or so helped it grow. My writer's brain took over, and I couldn't help asking myself who would send an old woman with dementia to the doctor alone with just a cab driver. Did she ever call him? Did he get stuck with her?

I don't know either of their names, but I want to take a moment to thank that gruff cab driver and the sweet, funny old woman he brought into my life that day. My mind has filled in the story quite nicely.

Thanks also to my publisher, Amanda Bostic, at HarperCollins Christian Publishing, and her predecessor Daisy Hutton, who saw the humor and fun in this book idea and allowed me to go for it, even though it's not like anything else I've written for them. The actual experience made for a good pitch, and they "got it" instantly. And I'm so grateful for Dave Lambert, who has edited most of my books for over twenty years, and Ellen Tarver, who has copyedited them for a decade or so. Both of these people are my crutches, and without them, I feel very insecure.

Thanks to Jodi Hughes, who takes the book the rest of the way through the printed stage, and Kristen Ingebretson, who creates my covers. Thanks to Paul Fisher and Allison Carter who do magic with marketing and publicity to get the word out about each of my novels. There are many others I've forgotten or whose names I don't know, but I'm infinitely grateful to them for all the things they do to get this book into your hands.

Finally, I want to thank my husband, Ken, who is my constant support system and the love of my life. He lives out the concept of dying to himself every single day, even when I'm not dying to mine. He bears with me in all my neurotic weirdness, and he arranges all within his control to make it possible for me to keep writing. He's a living illustration of how much I'm loved by God, because he models that love to me on a daily basis. I love him madly even though I don't always demonstrate it.

Discussion Questions

1. Sydney sends her grandmother to the doctor in a cab. Was that the right decision? What would you have done in her position?

2. Finn's day—and his life—is changed when he gets stuck with Miss Callie. What do you learn about his true character from his reaction to her?

3. Sydney is doing things she hates in order to keep her job. When is it time to cut your losses and risk what you've worked hard for?

4. What does Sydney learn about herself from her encounters with Finn?

5. What does Finn learn about himself from his encounters with Sydney?

6. When Finn and Sydney are looking for Callie, how does their relationship change? Does losing Callie help them find themselves?

7. What made this a merry Christmas for Finn, despite his reluctance to participate?

8. Why are Sydney and Finn right for each other? Could they have found true love without the intervention of God . . . and Callie?

9. How do forgiveness and redemption play into this story?

Terri Blackstock loves to hear from readers!
Contact her via social media or snail mail and
be sure to sign up for her newsletter!

www.TerriBlackstock.com
https://www.facebook.com/tblackstock

ZONDERVAN®
.com

DON'T MISS TERRI'S *USA TODAY* BESTSELLING SERIES, IF I RUN!

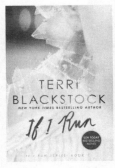
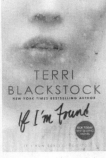
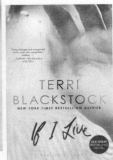

"Boiling with secrets, nail-biting suspense, and exquisitely developed characters, [*If I Run*] is a story that grabs hold and never lets go."
—COLLEEN COBLE, *USA TODAY* bestselling author of the Hope Beach and Lavender Tides series

Available in print, e-book, and audio!

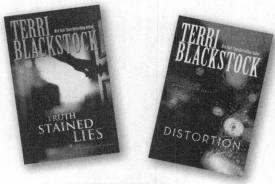
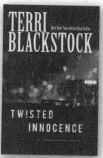

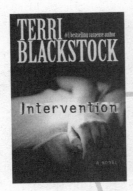
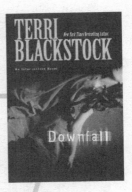
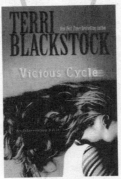

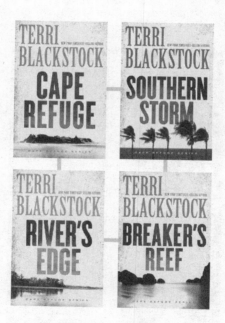

About the Author

PHOTO BY DERYLL STEGALL

Terri Blackstock has sold over seven million books worldwide and is a *New York Times* and *USA TODAY* bestselling author. She is the author of *If I Run, If I'm Found*, and *If I Live*, as well as such series as Cape Refuge, Newpointe 911, Intervention, and Restoration.

Visit her website at TerriBlackstock.com
Facebook: tblackstock
Twitter: @terriblackstock